# Montana RAIN

## JOSIE JADE

MONTANA RAIN: RESTING WARRIOR RANCH

# Chapter 1

**Cole Phillips**

CHICAGO WAS THE WORST.

Not only was it cold, but the people weren't friendly. Downtown was confusing, and the wind chill in this city was nothing short of damned ridiculous.

Then again, I doubted there was any city I would be happy in right now, because wherever it was? It was effectively banishment. I got sent here because there was extra desk space in the field office. Literally.

But it didn't matter. In a week, I wouldn't have to be here anymore. I wasn't sure who was more relieved that I suggested I take administrative leave while everything with Jones was resolved. Me, or the entire Federal Bureau of Investigation.

It didn't really matter that I'd saved lives or taken a bullet in the thigh while taking down Simon Derine; I was the agent who didn't notice his own partner was the scum of the earth. If I couldn't even recognize that, how was I supposed to be a functioning agent? How was anyone else supposed to want to partner with me when I clearly wasn't capable of what should have been basic common sense?

My stomach twisted, and I ran a hand over my face, the discomfort in my gut now familiar. I couldn't go long without the same track of thoughts running through my mind. Which was why I didn't want to be here anymore.

I needed to get away and be by myself for a while. And more importantly, be *out of sight* of the FBI while people either forgot about me or used the evidence to decide what they thought. My active presence wasn't helping anyone.

Reaching down, I rubbed my thigh. It had been more than a year since I'd been shot, but it still ached from time to time. Especially when it was cold. Which made me feel absolutely ancient, and I hated it. My doctors said it was normal, and my therapist said it was psychosomatic, brought on by all the guilt I harbored around the situation.

Because in my head, I didn't deserve to be healed when I could have stopped it all so much earlier. He was probably right, but I didn't need a therapist to tell me that. I needed someone to invent a time machine so I could go back and figure out what Jones was up to when it would have made a real difference.

Did I need to go to therapy?

Yes. I knew enough about post-traumatic stress to know I should be going, if only to sort out the myriad of complicated feelings I had about what had happened. But I wasn't going. Because the only thing I thought about while in my therapist's office wasn't figuring out my shit.

Instead, I thought about another, different therapist, with red hair, a killer body, and a tongue that could cut as sharply as a blade.

And the things I thought about had nothing to do with therapy.

*Physical* therapy, maybe.

I took a sip of my beer and looked around the bar of the hotel, the one good thing about being here. The Bureau put me up in a gorgeous hotel, and it was nice, because no one questioned you at hotel bars. Everyone was passing through, and the people on staff weren't the neighborhood, "Tell me your life story, stranger" type of bartenders.

Thank fuck.

A group of people came up beside me, clustering around the couple of empty barstools. The lanyards around their necks gave them away. There must have been a conference in the hotel. Poor bastards. Coming here now must be miserable. Late fall and early winter in Chicago so far had been nothing but wind, cold rain, and early snow. And not the good kind of snow. If I wanted snow, I wanted it to *snow*.

They ordered drinks, a couple of them taking the stools next to me and forcing me to move over in order not to be touching them.

"It was better last year." A man's voice cut through above the others. He had one of those voices that naturally resonated, but his tone also told me he wanted to be heard and noticed. "They should have had you speak again, Westerfield."

My ears perked up at the name. It was a coincidence—it had to be. Just because the elusive redhead who filled my thoughts far more than she should was also named Westerfield... It was a common name. Right?

Laughter sounded from all around the group, and they split into side discussions. But one laugh seemed to break through the rest, low and rich, and so fucking familiar, it made me sit up and pay attention.

"Thank you for the compliment, but I admit I was relieved not to be asked this year. It's fun and everything, but I don't miss the pressure of being a speaker."

Suddenly, I wasn't cold. Warm summer air filled my mind,

along with the faint thump of nearby music in that trademark Montana silence.

*"We shouldn't be doing this. I shouldn't be doing this."*

*I slipped a hand behind her neck and pulled her into me again, pinning her body against my car. "Should and shouldn't are overrated."*

*Rayne laughed. "You can't say things like that. You're part of the FBI."*

*"I'm not wearing a badge right now," I said quietly. "All I'm thinking about is this—and you."*

*I had no chance of keeping my lips off this woman. When I saw her the other day, I'd been so startled I'd nearly frozen in my tracks. No one had ever bowled me over at first sight before, and now that I'd spent the whole night looking at her, I wasn't sure anyone would do it ever again.*

*Leaning in, I kissed her. She tasted like whiskey and cherry lip gloss…and something deeper and sweeter that was absolutely her alone. The tiny moan in her throat was enough to undo me.*

"Still…" The brash man was still talking. "Your talk last year about PTSD was one of the best. I still use it every day with my clients. Not a single session this year even held a candle to it. I'd wager to say some of them were useless."

I glanced over just in time to confirm I was right. Rayne Westerfield was sitting not even ten feet from me, now frowning at the asshole who was making his displeasure known.

"There's always something worth learning, Arnold. Take some time and go back over your notes. I'm sure some things will pop out."

I smirked and took a sip of my beer. The man hadn't noticed the nearly undetectable put-down—that she'd called him by his first name instead of his last name. Hell, he probably thought it was an amazing thing, and he was now on a first-name basis with Rayne. Not that she wasn't giving him the same level of respect he gave her.

"Sure," he laughed. "That'll happen. I didn't take notes in any of these sessions."

Rayne stood, and I watched her from the corner of my eye. "That's a pity. I thought some of them were very informative. And considering three of the people who gave sessions today are within hearing distance, I would think carefully about how much more of an ass you want to make of yourself." She looked around the circle. "It was good to see you all, but I'd like to say hello to my family before I catch my flight in the morning."

There were murmured goodbyes, and *Arnold's* face was bright red. He'd been trying to impress her and flatter her, and it had backfired spectacularly.

Turning, I slipped off my barstool and waited for her to pass. "Is there anyone else you'd be willing to say hello to?"

Rayne froze, and she took a long, slow breath before looking up at me.

There it was. The invisible connection between us sprang to life, like a magnet was in my chest, pointed straight at her.

Her eyes widened, like she couldn't believe I was really standing here. I couldn't believe it either, because the two of us meeting at a hotel in Chicago seemed pretty unlikely. But then again, plenty of things in my life so far were unlikely. Running into the woman I'd been thinking about for a year was honestly pretty low on the list.

"Cole Phillips," she said, tone intentionally neutral. "What are you doing here?"

"Join me for a drink, and I'll tell you."

She laughed once. "Thanks, but no thanks."

"Rayne." I took a step forward. "I'm sorry. You don't know how sorry I am. I've wanted to apologize to you forever—"

"Then why haven't you?" Her eyes blazed with fury. "We have technology now, Cole. Phones and email. If you really wanted to apologize, you could have."

She wasn't wrong, but I honestly didn't know what to say, because I wasn't clear on what had happened. I assumed it was because of Simon and the Riders and, just like the FBI, not knowing my partner was a piece of shit.

But that wasn't the beginning of it. The beginning was me kissing her and feeling like I could finally *breathe* for the first time in my life before she'd pushed me away and said she couldn't.

"I am sorry," I said. "I'm not sure what I did, which was why I didn't reach out. I…" I scratched the back of my neck. "I should have anyway, because I haven't been able to stop thinking about you."

"Really?" Rayne stepped in closer to me. "You haven't been able to stop thinking about me for a year?"

"It's the truth." This close, I could smell her sweet cherry lip gloss. I remembered it like it was yesterday. That, and her perfume, which I swore made her skin smell like honey. This woman was made to undo me.

"You were an ass," she said. "To all my friends. To my client. You were the reason Daniel was shot."

"Yes." I accepted responsibility for all of it. Jones was the one who did the shit with using Emma's name and got Daniel shot, but it didn't matter. I should have questioned more, and I didn't. "I've cleared the air with them," I said, closing the last bit of distance separating us. "But Daniel was shot *after* I kissed you."

Rayne's cheeks turned pink, and I craved that color. I craved her being flustered. Because whatever made her push me away that night? It sure as hell wasn't me being a dick. I had been one, and I owned it. My desire to catch Simon Derine outweighed everything else in my view, and I'd let it blind me.

"That was a mistake," Rayne said softly. "An error in judgment."

6

"Was it?"

"Yes."

The breathy tone of her voice told me she was lying. But I wouldn't do anything about it. Not for the moment. Soon enough, I'd have more chances.

"Okay, Rayne. But for what it's worth, I am sorry. For everything. It was good to see you."

A flood of people suddenly came through the doors. Sports fans. Must be a game tonight. Rayne stepped back and looked at me with more heat than I think she realized. "I'm glad I won't have to see you again, Cole."

She disappeared into the crowd exactly as she meant to, and I went back to my beer. I smiled. If Rayne was glad she didn't have to see me again, she was going to be *really* upset when she found out Garnet Bend was where I was spending the next four months.

Downing the last of my drink, I tossed cash on the bar and headed back to my room. The sooner I could get out of here, the better. For both the FBI and for me.

MONTANA WASN'T a place I saw myself, but seeing Rayne again? This was going to be fun.

# Chapter 2

**Rayne Westerfield**

I HAD TO BE HALLUCINATING.

As a therapist, I was pretty sure I wasn't, but I *hoped* I was hallucinating. Because Cole Phillips was here.

In Chicago.

Staring down at me just like he had last year, seconds before he had me pressed up against his car and put his lips on mine in the best kiss of my damn life.

And I couldn't do it. Because Cole Phillips made me feel out of control, and that was absolutely unacceptable. The reasons I gave him were bullshit and we both knew it, but this was Chicago. In the morning, I was getting on a plane to Montana, and he'd go back to whatever mission he was currently on. That would be the end of it.

The surge of people coming in the doors of the hotel lobby distracted both of us, and I took the opportunity to step back and put some space between us. "I'm glad I won't have to see you again, Cole."

I could have imagined it, but I thought he smiled before I fully turned around. And like hell was I going to admit what that kind of smile did to me.

I turned, taking my coat from over my arm and putting it on. Chicago wasn't as cold as Montana in general, but the wind chill was both legendary and brutal. I was going to need my coat, even on the short walk to Mom and Ava's apartment.

All the breath left me as someone ran into me. A woman, definitely not dressed for the chill. Long dark hair and panic in her eyes. She was pressed up against me for only a second before she clawed away from me and sprinted through the crowd deeper into the hotel.

I lost her. Enough people were milling around the lobby now that it was too dense to see, even with someone sprinting.

Turning back to the doors, I saw three men burst through them and start to look around. Like they were chasing someone. Someone who was running. I noted the suits they wore, which contrasted with the intensity with which they were looking.

I might not know what was going on, but like hell was I going to let someone be chased, regardless. The men had slowed down and had waded into the crowd. Pushing my way through in the opposite direction of the bar, I edged around until I reached the concierge desk. "Excuse me."

The woman looked up, and her eyes locked on my badge from the conference. Instantly, her face transformed into a smile. "Yes, how can I help you?"

"Three men just came into the lobby chasing a woman." I pointed them out in the crowd. "I don't know where she went, but I didn't want to just let it happen."

"Yeah." Her eyes went wide. She grabbed the radio that sat on her desk. "I need security in the lobby."

The thing squawked. "We're here. What do you need?"

"Come to the desk."

A couple of guys pushed through the crowd, and I'd bet they were off-duty cops from the way they carried themselves. I pointed out the three men—now deep into the lobby crowd—and watched as security found them and escorted them out of the hotel.

The woman was still nowhere to be found. I gave her description to the concierge and checked the lobby bathroom, but there was no sign of her. Whatever happened to her and whatever she was running from, I hoped it didn't catch up with her.

Finally, I left and made the ten-minute walk back to the downtown apartment my mother and sister shared. I unlocked the door, trying to be quiet since it was getting late. Ava would probably already be asleep.

Instead, I was greeted with the low sound of sitcom laughter and all the lights on. Mom and Ava sat in the living room, watching a show. "What are you two doing up? I thought you'd be asleep by now."

Ava rolled her eyes. "Like we'd go to sleep on your last night here."

She was on the couch and not in her chair, settled in and comfortable. My mom, on the other hand, was exhausted. I saw in her eyes that she was drooping and staying awake for Ava's sake. She probably had a packed day tomorrow, but she was doing this for her.

Familiar guilt clogged my throat, and I forced a smile at the two of them. "Sorry I'm so late. I meant to leave a little earlier, but there was a little chaos at the hotel." I shrugged off my coat and shoes before snuggling in between them on the couch. "Girl ran into me, seemed like she was being chased. I stayed to make sure the guys who were running after her were taken out of the building."

"Oh my goodness," Mom breathed. "I hope she's all right."

"Me too."

I put my hand around my sister's shoulders and pulled her closer. "How you holding up, squirt?"

She laughed once, even as she cuddled into me. "I'm twenty-eight, Rayne. I think you can give up calling me 'squirt.'"

"You'll always be a squirt to me," I said. The nickname came from when she was younger and tiny compared to the other kids. It stuck, even after the accident.

Ava sighed. "Fine." The way she said it, she was smiling. Far less annoyed about the nickname than she was letting on.

"When's your flight?" Mom asked.

"Ten. So, I'll be out of here by seven."

I didn't love the idea of being up so early, especially when my body was still an hour earlier on Montana time, but I was looking forward to getting home, even if there was guilt attached to that as well.

"When are you coming back to visit?" Ava asked.

"Well, Christmas for sure. So, it'll only be a couple months."

"Good."

Her body relaxed, and she sank into sleep almost immediately. I guess I was wrong about her being alert and awake. Slowly, I moved her, lifting her into her chair before wheeling her into her bedroom and putting her to bed. While I was here, I tried to give my mother a break from this.

Ava could argue all she wanted, but she was still small. I didn't have a problem lifting her in and out of her wheelchair, and I wasn't a woman known for physical strength.

I leaned against the wall in the living room. "She didn't seem that tired when I walked in."

"She'll always pretend for you, Rayne." Mom sighed and stood, gathering the cups off the coffee table before bringing them back to the kitchen. "I'm sorry you have to leave so soon."

"Yeah…" I pressed my lips together. "Sorry."

Mom laughed once. "Believe me, I get it. This time of year, things are usually slowing down. But at this rate, I'll be out straight through Christmas."

She was a lawyer. A defense attorney for any number of things. Which was why I knew staying up late was a sacrifice for both Ava and me. "How's she doing with Carly?"

"Carly's great," Mom said. "The best caretaker Ava's ever had. Honestly, things have been much easier with her around."

"If you need help with the money for it—"

"We're fine, Rayne." She smiled. "But thank you. If we need that kind of help, I'll ask for it."

"Promise?"

"Promise."

She looked at me, and that strange distance spun between us. I loved my mother, and she loved me. But there were things between us you couldn't ever take back and you couldn't get over, and in silences like this, I could feel it like a third person was standing in the room.

"Montana's good?"

"It is," I said with a smile. "Everyone is doing well. Finally."

We both chuckled. My family got a kick out of the stories that came out of Garnet Bend, whether it was laughing at the Resting Warrior alpacas or not quite believing so many bad things could happen to good people.

"I'm glad to hear it. We really do want to come visit sometime."

"Ava would love it," I said.

My family didn't understand my decision to leave the big city and establish a practice in the middle of nowhere. But I couldn't stay here. They might not get why, but Chicago was filled with bad memories and reminders of both failure and grief.

Not to mention the clear mountain air did wonders. It wasn't a cure-all like the people in the Regency era seemed to think when they sent sick people to be by the sea, but you couldn't doubt Montana had a therapeutic quality.

The sweetness that seemed to live in the air, and the silence that stretched on into infinity. A million and one stars because there weren't lights like here in Chicago. Everything about that place was something I loved.

Who knew? Maybe I was never meant to live in a city.

"Maybe next year?" I asked. "Spring or early summer? It's beautiful that time."

"If I start planning it now, I might be able to find the time," Mom said. She was grinning, because we both knew how crazy her schedule was and how quickly it filled up. But I'd keep reminding her.

She rinsed out the glasses she'd brought from the living room and wiped off her hands. "I am sorry to just leave you alone on your last night…"

"It's okay," I said. "You probably have an early morning."

"I do." She pulled me into a hug, and I sank into it. No one gave hugs like your mom. "I love you, Rayne. Even when you're so far away."

"I love you too, Mom."

We stood there for a minute, just enjoying the hug before she pulled away. "Say goodbye to me in the morning, okay? And let me know when you get home."

"I will."

She touched my cheek before going to her bedroom and shutting the door. In the living room, the sound of the sitcom still played, and I blew out a breath.

Sinking onto the couch, I let my head fall back and stared at the ceiling. No matter how many times I came home, it never seemed to get easier. The same awkwardness, the same elephant in the room, the same guilt I couldn't seem to shake, even though it was my *job* to help people through their problems.

I scrubbed my hands over my face. Someday, when I'd done enough good, maybe I'd find a way to help myself with my own.

## Chapter 3

**Cole**

I LOOKED out the window of the cabin and sighed.

This was a stupid idea.

I sat in the cabin I'd rented from a man who'd warned me that if I messed with his *stash* in the basement, he reserved the right to kick my ass. Daniel had laughed when I'd told him, but he didn't seem surprised.

When I left Chicago, I wanted to get here as quickly as possible. Resting Warrior was letting me rent a truck, and I was now just...here.

Bored out of my mind.

Who was I kidding? I'd known I would be bored, but I didn't anticipate the *bigness* of the silence here. It was honestly a bit freaky. Last time, I'd been so wrapped up in the case I didn't notice.

Still, the boredom was preferable. I needed to remember that. Being bored and going out of my mind alone was far better than being stuck behind a desk in a field office with everyone watching me.

They would do me the courtesy of pretending not to watch, but it still felt like living in the middle of a fishbowl.

I sighed and let my head fall back against the chair. Maybe this hadn't been the right place to come. It was mostly because of Daniel. He was the one who'd come to visit me in the hospital. The only one. We cleared the air after everything that went down with Simon.

My hand dropped to my thigh, rubbing the site of the bullet wound. It already ached a little more here, sensitive to the altitude and temperature.

Thankfully, the other Resting Warrior men had come around as well, and if we weren't on *good* terms, at least they weren't about to rip me open and string me up by my guts. During the next couple of months, I hoped I could undo some of the damage I'd done, because Rayne was right about one thing—I'd been a class A dick.

Then there was *that* reason I'd come here.

Rayne.

She was here.

I wanted to be close to her, just to see if there was any chance of giving the chemistry that was clearly between us a shot. If, at the end of my time here, she still hated my guts, then I'd learn to live with it. There was something about the woman I just couldn't shake.

Hell, if she weren't here, I didn't think I would have genuinely entertained staying in a cabin in the mountains for four months. Maybe I would have just gone to a beach house or an unfamiliar city. Not one of the most sparsely populated states in the US.

Leaning forward, I dropped my head into my hands. I was here, and that wasn't changing, so I needed to get used to things and get myself into a routine. First things first, I needed food. For all of Jimmy's bluster—his name was Jimmy, not Jim or James—the cabin wasn't exactly prepped for the end of the world.

The stash he'd warned me off was a decent size. Wood-burning generator, a satellite phone, some maps and cans of water, rope, and plenty of nonperishable food I wasn't permitted to touch. Not as extreme as I'd expected and not exactly a typical prepper, but I wasn't going to complain. The amount of money I paid to rent this place for four months wouldn't even cover the rent of an apartment for *one* month in Chicago or Seattle.

Might as well familiarize myself with the town and the stores. I knew my way roughly around from the last time, but it had been a while.

I laughed as I drove down the mountain. Time for me to brush up on my cooking skills too. Not like there was a lot of delivery out here, and I wasn't too proud to admit I had been more interested in my career than avoiding delivery fees for the last few years.

At least the cabin had a good fridge and freezer.

The September air had a bite to it. Not exactly cold, but the tingle of winter was in the air, hovering just out of reach. Like it was taunting everyone with how quickly it could make their lives miserable if it got the chance.

The main grocery store was great. I bought more food than I probably needed, with ambitions of teaching myself recipes that I'd wanted to learn for a long time. What else was I going to do?

I needed to get a library card. Check out some books. Get some practice filling the time.

"Phillips?"

The voice came from over my shoulder, and I turned from loading my groceries into the truck to find Jude and Liam from Resting Warrior standing there. "Hey."

"Daniel told us you'd gotten into town."

"Hunt me down to settle the score?" My tone was light, but I still wasn't on perfect terms with these guys, and I wanted to see how much I needed to worry.

Jude laughed. "No. We're all past that."

"Doesn't mean we won't give you shit," Liam said. "Because we absolutely will."

"I would expect nothing less."

Jude leaned against the back of the truck. "Getting settled in okay? That cabin is pretty far out."

The words didn't immediately come to mind. "It's...not what I'm used to. But in the end, it's probably a good thing."

"Things not going well back in Seattle?" Liam crossed his arms.

I shoved my hands into my pockets. When I'd come to get supplies I hadn't anticipated baring my soul, but I wasn't going to hide why I was here. Part of all of this had taught me I needed to own up to my shit. "They moved me to Chicago and sat me behind a desk." I shook my head. "No one trusts me enough to be my partner. They don't want me in the field, and the 'investigation' into everything that happened is taking so long, I'm wondering if they're trying to run out the clock on me. So I volunteered for administrative leave. I'll be bored as fuck, but at least I'll be bored without an audience."

Jude nodded once. "I understand that. Hard to get ahold of your own mind when you're aware of everyone else trying to get ahold of it for you."

"Yeah."

"Well," Liam said, "if you are that bored and have the time, come by the ranch. Maybe day after tomorrow? We've got a new building going up and can show you around more than we did last time."

The three of us chuckled. It was true; the farthest I'd been onto the ranch was the lodge, both last time and when I'd picked up the truck. "Sure. I'd like that."

"And," Jude said, "Lena will kick my ass if I don't invite you to family dinner that night."

I went stiff. Hanging out with the guys was one thing. We could find ways to relate to one another. All of them had been SEALs too. But their wives and girlfriends? To them, I was probably still the man who put Daniel in danger, just like Rayne thought. The man who unreasonably risked Emma Derine's life for the sake of his mission. "That might be too soon?"

Liam waved a hand. "Nah. Daniel and Emma have both forgiven you, and the rest of us followed. Putting something off doesn't make it less awkward."

Damn. He had a point there, but I felt called out.

"Emma and Daniel had their son a few months ago," Jude said. "I'm sure they'd love for you to meet him."

I held up my hands in surrender. "All right, you win. But if someone wants me to leave, I'm not going to force my presence on anyone."

"Fair enough." Liam clapped me on the shoulder. "But that won't happen."

A flash of red caught my eye, and I zeroed in on the redhead across the street.

*Rayne.*

Even from this distance, she took my breath away. It had been forever since I'd seen her hair in the sun like that. Copper and darker tones of reddish-brown. A bright-green shirt that I wanted to see up close, because I already knew she'd look stunning in it.

Suddenly I became aware that both Liam and Jude were staring at me, at least ten full seconds of silence had passed, and they could see where I was looking.

Liam smirked. "That's interesting."

I looked at them both. "Please don't tell her I'm here. When she finds out, I want it to be from me."

Jude shrugged. "Sure."

"I'll see you guys in a couple of days?"

"Looking forward to it."

Loading up the rest of the groceries into the back of my truck, I waited until Rayne wasn't in sight walking on the street before I started the engine and headed back to my mountain of solitude.

Something fiery lived in the space between us. I wanted— no, I *needed*—to figure out what it was. But first, I had to make sure she knew I was here. The best I could hope for was that it wasn't a completely unpleasant surprise.

## Chapter 4

**Rayne**

I SIGHED after the last client left, glad it was a short day. For the past few days, my head had been in a daze I couldn't seem to shake. Like something was suddenly off, and I couldn't figure out what.

Since I'd come back from Chicago, I'd felt restless, and I hated it. Garnet Bend was my home now. A sleepy, or sometimes not so sleepy, town. I loved my job, I had great friends, and even my house was a haven I'd taken pains to create.

So why did I suddenly feel like there was a piece missing?

Closing my eyes and blowing out a breath, I tried to sift through the feeling. I was overdue for one of my own therapy appointments, and it would probably help. The guilt that came up every time I went home was still palpable and maybe was why I still felt like this.

*Liar.*

Most therapists went to therapy. It wasn't easy taking on the emotions and problems of others all day. I loved it, and guiding people through both their trauma and everyday struggles made me feel like I was doing good in the world—and mitigated that pesky guilt.

But it was still a weight I had to bear most days.

And yet, that part of me knew I was lying to myself about what was bothering me—and about when it had started. For a long time, I'd been able to ignore it, but in Chicago, when I saw *him*…

*Cole leaned in and kissed me. Suddenly, it felt like my body was on fire, and I didn't dare move and break the moment. He had my body trapped between his and the car, and I felt every hard inch of him. Desire built in my blood. I couldn't get enough of him.*

*I'd never been kissed like this. Like he was kissing* all *of me and not just my mouth. Like Cole was pouring starlight directly through my lips. I moaned, unable to stop myself.*

*Stark clarity and guilt slammed into me like a train. I'd hurt him. People who loved me got hurt, and as much as I wanted to let this man pull me into his car and take me home, I couldn't let him close. If anything happened to him because of me, I wouldn't survive it.*

*Deep down where my soul rested, I knew he was different. Because of that, we had to stop. "I can't," I gasped, pushing against his chest. "I can't."*

*Cole was just as breathless. "Rayne—"*

*"Goodbye, Cole." I turned and walked away, feeling cold even in the warm summer night.*

I loved my job and my home, but I was also lonely.

Fuck, why couldn't I be attracted to someone who was good for me? Someone boring and steady, not someone who put their life at risk regularly.

The fear was irrational, but most fears of this kind were, and it was so deep, I didn't know if it would ever go away.

Time to go home and just relax. Order a pizza and sit on the couch watching TV until I was too tired to move. I rarely did that, and it sounded perfect.

"Hey, Rayne?"

I startled at Nancy's voice, thinking she'd already gone. "Yes?"

"Sorry." She poked her head into the office. She held a small white card in her hand. "This was leaned up against the door outside. I didn't want it to get lost."

"Oh." I frowned. "Thank you."

She handed it to me, and this time, I heard the front door close behind her. The little card in my hand was like one you might get with flowers. And inside, I saw neat, stark hand-writing.

RAYNE,

I'M *in town for a while, and I wanted you to hear it from me. I'll be at Montana Jewels coffee, so there's more privacy from our Resting Warrior friends. I hope to see you and explain.*

-COLE PHILLIPS

MY HEART POUNDED in my chest. This wasn't real. It couldn't be real. There was no way Cole was suddenly in Garnet Bend like I'd manifested him out of thin air.

This had to be a practical joke from one of the girls. I'd mentioned to them that I'd run into Cole in Chicago when I grabbed my coffee yesterday.

But what if it wasn't a joke?

My stomach tightened. If he was actually here—

I closed my eyes. Even if it was a practical joke, I would risk being laughed at, because I couldn't stay away. It was an impossible contradiction. I meant what I'd said to him in the hotel about being glad I wouldn't see him anymore. But that was because I wanted it so desperately, I needed him far away.

I was locking the office behind myself and walking toward Montana Jewels before I could fully register the decision to do so. Nerves swam in my gut. Maybe pizza wasn't going to be a good idea after all. I'd see when I got to the shop.

I turned the corner and looked at the shop, and my whole body went rigid. It was him. He was sitting at one of the small tables near the front windows, reading a book and sipping coffee like he did it every day.

He wasn't in a suit now. The dark jeans and blue Henley suited him. The sleeves of his shirt were pushed up, and I almost felt the need to avert my eyes. Forearm porn was one hundred percent real, and Cole Phillips embodied it.

Now that I knew he was here, I wasn't sure if I was furious or relieved. Furious because he was inexplicably here, and relieved because there was something between us, even if I wished there weren't.

I pushed into the store and his eyes lifted to mine. Just like the hotel all over again. He pinned me to the spot with his gaze, and what I saw there shook me. It wasn't victory or joy or even gloating.

It was hope.

"Rayne."

"I'm just…" I cleared my throat. "I'm going to get a drink."

He nodded. "Okay."

I ordered a latte and wrapped my arms around myself while I waited for the barista to make it. I should walk away right now and forget Cole Phillips ever existed.

But I *was* lonely, and even I wasn't strong enough to be self-less all the time.

"Here you go," the barista said, handing me the drink.

"Thanks."

The chair across from him was empty, and his book was now closed. I sat down, and I had absolutely no idea what to say. All I knew was we had a force between us that felt physical, and every time I saw him, it was harder to ignore it.

A flicker of a smile crossed his face before it disappeared. "I wasn't sure you would come."

"Me either."

He chuckled. "Glad I won the internal battle."

Irritation rose under my skin. That was what Cole did to me, along with the alarming chemistry. He got under my skin. "What are you doing here?"

I saw him make the smallest wince. "I live here for the moment. I'm on administrative leave from the Bureau, and Daniel had a line on a cabin I could rent to get away from things for a while."

"Daniel spoke to you?"

"Some people do still occasionally stoop to talk to me."

I glared at him, and he smirked.

He *lived* here. I honestly didn't know how to feel about it.

"Why didn't you say anything in Chicago?"

Cole tilted his head. "When was I supposed to do that? When you were insulting me, when you were telling me that kissing me was a mistake, or when you said you never wanted to see me again?" His tone teased.

"Maybe saying things like that is the reason I was glad you were gone." I stood, not able to do this. Cole made me too confused. My instinct was to spar back with him, but if I did, I would pull him closer, and I couldn't.

*I couldn't.*

"Wait, Rayne," he said, his voice dropping into a softer register, and he sighed. "I wanted you to know I was in town, and I didn't want it to be a surprise. Clearly…" He hesitated and shook his head. "Clearly, seeing me in Chicago unexpectedly wasn't fun for you."

He stood, and I was immediately reminded of how tall he was. How built. How I knew what his body felt like from those brief, stirring moments when he'd had me pressed up against his car.

Cole took the receipt he was using as a bookmark out of his book and strode to the counter, borrowing their pen and scribbling something on the back before he returned to me.

"But there's something between us, Rayne. You know it, and I know it. I won't pressure you, but I'm here. For now." He handed me the receipt, and I saw his number written on the back of it. "If you want to call me, I'll answer."

He picked up his book and his coffee and left the shop, walking down the sidewalk away from me. I saw him get into a truck, and his eyes locked with mine before he pulled out.

Once he disappeared, I blew out a breath. What the hell had just happened? And why did the receipt in my hand now feel like the center of the world?

# Chapter 5

**Cole**

THE BARE BONES structure of the building in front of me was impressive. Clearly much bigger than any of the other current buildings, it would be two stories and have more than enough space for what they wanted to do with it.

It made sense, expanding the operation. The crew here was changing. From what I understood, when Resting Warrior had started, the men who made up the main staff were all single. Now, none of them were. Two had children, and I suspected more would soon be on the way.

When everyone around you was entering a different phase of life with different priorities, bringing in more people to help continue what you started was the smart move.

If I was honest with myself, Resting Warrior made me envious. The brotherhood these men had and the seamlessness with which they worked toward their mission was what I'd wanted when I'd joined the FBI.

No one needed to mention how that had turned out.

"Have you hired anyone yet?"

"No," Daniel said. "We're dealing with some permit issues on the construction itself, which is why it's paused. Didn't want to go forward with hiring anyone when we're not sure of the finish date."

I nodded. "Makes sense."

"But hopefully once it's open, we'll have physical therapists on staff, so we can take people earlier in their journey and focus on both the physical *and* mental part of their healing."

"People could definitely use it." I'd gotten lucky. When I went into the SEALs, I came out unscathed. My trauma came from other places, and I was still dealing with it. But I knew plenty of men in all branches of military and government service who could be helped by a place like Resting Warrior. "You're going to have a waiting list."

He chuckled. "We already do. But some of that will be fixed soon."

"How so?"

He nodded toward where the rest of the guys were clustered nearer to the actual structure. "Lucas, Evelyn, and their daughter will be moving off the property soon, and we'll be turning their house into a guest house with a few rooms for the more mobile guests. And another one of our staff, Mara, is also moving off the property."

"Is anyone staying?"

"I am, with Emma and Tyson. Someone's got to live here, and we just built our house. I'm not keen on leaving it so soon."

I felt a pang in my chest. "How's your son?"

The smile on Daniel's face made up for the fact that it was overcast today. "He's incredible. A little over three months now. You'll meet him tonight."

We walked back toward the group of men. "Are you sure it will be all right?"

"I am." His voice brooked no room for argument.

Well, then. Couldn't argue with that tone.

"If you guys need any help around the place, it's not like I'll be busy."

Daniel smirked. "Already bored?"

"*God*, yes."

His laugh drew the attention of the others, and he clapped me on the shoulder. "Well, we can always use help. Especially with us rearranging things and such. We can talk about it in a couple of days."

"Thanks. I think I'll appreciate just getting out of the cabin."

"No problem."

The others watched as we approached, and Noah was grinning. "There's one thing we haven't shown Phillips yet."

"What's that?" Daniel asked.

"The gym."

Something about those two words meant more than I understood. "Is that code for where you bury the bodies?"

Liam laughed under his breath. "No, I think that's Noah's way of saying there are some who want to spar with you."

I raised an eyebrow and looked around. No one disagreed. "I'm down for some sparring." It wasn't entirely unexpected. Some fault lines of tension still stretched between me and the group. If sparring with them and potentially getting my ass kicked cleared any of the air, I would do it.

"Seriously, though," Lucas said as the group of us began to walk. "Are things okay with you? Banishing yourself to a cabin in the woods for a few months is usually a sign something's wrong."

Shrugging, I shook my head. "Hell if I know. Ask me again in a week. My head's everywhere right now."

He accepted the answer, and it was true. Simply seeing the community here up close was enough to make me question anything. It looked *easy*. I knew it wasn't, but this was the kind of place that worked hard to keep everything out in the open. They had rules for communication and weren't afraid to check one another when they needed. And, as I had experienced firsthand, they weren't afraid to protect what was theirs.

The gym was a large building behind the main lodge, and bigger than I expected. Harlan shoved open the door, and I did a double take. This wasn't a building with a couple of punching bags. This was a fucking *gym*. Punching bags, weights, machines, and a huge area with mats for sparring. Even lockers lined the far wall.

"Damn, you guys don't mess around."

"You've seen why," Grant said quietly.

Yes. I had.

"Feel free to use this whenever," Daniel said. "Though I'm sure you could run up and down the mountain too." I winced, and his eyes dropped to my leg. "Still?"

"It's fine. Not sure it'll ever be the same, but it's doing all right."

Noah tossed me some gym shorts. We were about the same size. "They're clean, I swear."

"Well, I'm not going to smell them to find out."

He shoved down a laugh, and I held out a hand. "I know we're all…mostly good, but since you're all here, and I haven't said it to anyone but Daniel, I'm sorry. I was a jackass and a dick to every single one of you, and my reasons for it don't matter. Thank you for letting me spend some time here."

The words hung in the air, but something significant relaxed. I felt the shift, and Grant nodded once, meeting my gaze. "Accepted."

I pulled off my jacket and shirt, followed by my jeans and shoes. The borrowed shorts went on, and by the time I was finished, three guys were almost ready. "I hope you're not planning to spar with me all at once."

"Nah." Jude tossed me the tape for my hands. "But they all want a go."

Noah, Grant, and Harlan all looked ready to spar, and considering they were all different builds, it wasn't going to be easy. I sat down on the mats and began to tape my hands. "It's been a while. You'll have to take it easy on me."

Harlan grinned. "Are you saying a member of the esteemed Federal Bureau of Investigation isn't ready for anything at all times?"

"Not ones who've been behind a desk for a year," I laughed. "But don't worry, I can still kick your ass."

"I hope so."

Good. It was the answer I wanted. If they weren't looking for me to let them win, then things really were fine. This wasn't just about getting a free chance to beat the hell out of me; it was only sparring.

Satisfaction settled in my chest.

This, I could do.

Noah was the first one on the mat with me, and we were well matched. He jumped toward me, aiming to land a punch that would have put me on the floor. But I moved out of the way. He wouldn't get me so easily.

Fuck, this felt good. I hadn't sparred like this in forever. Since before I'd come to Resting Warrior the first time. It dawned on me as I ducked under Noah's arm, that was the point.

They saw what I needed and offered it. Because if I was out here, hiding in a cabin, I needed an outlet for *something*.

The realization slamming down onto me like one of those two-ton weights from the cartoons distracted me, and I was suddenly on the floor without knowing how I got there.

I swore, and Noah helped me to my feet. "Not bad, Phillips."

"Let me get another chance once I'm in practice again."

"Done."

I looked around, and Grant was gone. Harlan tipped his head toward the door. "His wife called, needed something. You've got me."

Harlan had both height and weight on me. But I was warmed up now. At least I had a decent shot. This time, I struck first. I was faster, but his advantages made him hit harder.

Incredibly, it was a more even fight. We went back and forth, our energy draining, until Harlan finally made the mistake I was waiting for. Stepping inside his guard, I swept his legs out from under him, and he went down.

"Fucking finally," Lucas said, and all of us were laughing. "Thought you both would be fighting all the way through dinner."

I reached down and helped Harlan up. We locked eyes, and I saw respect there. This had helped both them and me.

"Speaking of dinner," a feminine voice said. "It's about time for that." A short, curvy woman with streaks of color in her hair crossed over to Jude. He dwarfed her, but the love between them was so tangible it was magnetic. He curled himself around her, and I looked away.

Toward the door.

Jude's fiancée hadn't come to retrieve us alone.


RAYNE WAS STANDING at the door, staring straight at me.

# Chapter 6

**Rayne**

COLE PHILLIPS STOOD in front of me, shirtless and glistening with sweat.

I would be a liar if I said I hadn't imagined him with less clothing than I'd seen him in, but an imaginary image and a very *not* imaginary reality were completely different. My mouth was dry, and I couldn't seem to take my eyes off him, nor he me.

"Get cleaned up and come inside. We're not waiting," Lena called, spinning away from Jude, her cheeks flushed from the way he'd just kissed her.

"Come on." Lena turned me and looped her arm through mine, forcing me to break the stare.

I waited until we were outside. "Did you guys plan this? Cole and me?"

Lena laughed. "I didn't. Promise. But don't discount the men in this scenario. Now that they're becoming husbands and fathers, all of them are acting like mother hens and match-makers. I didn't even know you were coming."

"No, it was Evie who called and asked me to come."

The Resting Warrior family dinner had been rotating through people's houses. But since Lucas and Evie were getting ready to move, the dinner was at the lodge, the way it always used to be.

"She could be in on it," Lena said. "Or Lucas. Either way, I approve."

I rolled my eyes. "Of course you do."

"What's the real reason you don't want to be around him?"

Pressing my lips together, I said nothing. Right before family dinner wasn't when I wanted to get into all the details of why that would be a monumentally disastrous idea.

But my mind also had trouble recalling what any of those reasons were when all I could see was Cole's naked chest and remember what it felt like to be pinned against his body. Now my mind could put the two things together and imagine what it might be like to be pinned *without* the clothing.

I was so screwed.

"There are lots of reasons."

Lena snorted with laughter. "Sure. Okay, Rayne."

"He's arrogant, and he was awful to everyone." She pushed open the back door to the lodge. "But we'll discuss it later. I don't want him thinking I'm talking about him."

"Okay." She threw a look over her shoulder that told me she didn't believe me even for a second.

I didn't believe myself either.

The main room of the lodge was all chatter, and I smiled over at the fire where Emma sat with Tyson, chatting with Evie, who watched little Avery, who was starting to pull herself up on the furniture. Grant was helping Cori set the table, and the whole scene was one of joy and warmth.

Only a couple minutes passed before the men came in from the gym, and Cole was thankfully dressed in normal clothes, with a shirt. But he still stared at me like we were locked in some sort of trance.

"Who won?" Grant called.

"Noah kicked my ass the first time," Cole said, still looking at me. "But I got Harlan."

"We're both going to have rematches."

Emma came over, Tyson in her arms, and Cole stiffened. A smile slipped on his face, but I noticed the tension. "Hello, Emma."

"It's weird to call you Cole and not 'Agent Phillips,'" she said.

He chuckled. "It's weird for me too. I'm not used to being called by my first name."

"We'll still call you Phillips," Jude said. "Just to make sure you get your fix."

We all took seats, and the guys began bringing food over to the table. These dinners had a natural balance. When it rotated throughout the houses, whoever hosted and cooked never had to clean. If the women prepared, the men served. A silent and continuous agreement that everyone was in this together, and nothing was assumed.

"Okay," Lena said as soon as everyone sat down. "I can't possibly hold this in any longer."

Jude chuckled and pulled her into his side, kissing the top of her head. They were so in love, it was inspiring to see. Even now, she closed her eyes, accepting the affection. The gnawing hole in my chest that I'd identified yesterday ached. Loneliness.

Watching all my friends be happy and fulfilled was incredibly satisfying. And also difficult.

I looked away from Jude and Lena to find Cole looking at me again, like he knew exactly what was going through my mind. His mouth turned up into the tiniest smirk, and I looked away.

"We've set a date," Lena said. "This spring."

The table erupted in cheers, and everyone had smiles on their faces. In our minds, Lena and Jude were basically married. But their wedding was going to be the celebration of the century for Garnet Bend.

"Now," Cori said, leaning in and reaching for the bottle of wine in the middle of the table. "The wedding is one thing. But the honeymoon is another. Have you thought about where you want to go?"

Lena laughed. "At this point, I'll be happy to go wherever because I haven't been anywhere in so long. I was jealous of Rayne when she was in Chicago. Maybe we'll go there."

"Take it from me," Cole said. "Don't go to Chicago on your honeymoon."

"Because you've been on so many honeymoons?" The words snapped out of my mouth so fast, the entire room had gone quiet before I fully processed I'd said them.

Cole's eyes found mine, that maddening smirk on his face. He liked getting under my skin, the bastard. "Not many honeymoons," he said. "None, actually. But having spent the last few months in Chicago, I feel qualified to say it's not a good place for a honeymoon."

I struggled not to roll my eyes. "It's not the traditional beach getaway, but there're some amazing things in Chicago. Museums, architecture, Navy Pier, Millennium Park, *incredible* pizza."

He leaned back in his chair. "Putting aside the problematic nature of the Bean and its creator, I didn't say Chicago wasn't a good place to visit. I said it wasn't a good place to go on your *honeymoon*." Cole glanced at Jude. "If I'm choosing a place to go on my honeymoon, I'm choosing a place that's beautiful but doesn't have tourist attractions, so I don't feel guilty when I choose not to spend as much time…outside."

I flushed even as everyone laughed. Right this second, I was so aware of Cole and his body, it felt like I was on fire. His gaze burned into mine, my breath going short.

No one had ever affected me like this, and I didn't know what to do. Because people didn't spar with me. Not like this.

"I think you can have a good honeymoon anywhere. It's all about who you're with, right? If you were miserable, then maybe it's the company you kept."

I saw the trap a second before he sprung it. "Does that include when we ran into each other?"

Someone gasped. Everyone was watching us like a championship tennis match. I needed to defuse this. Family dinner wasn't the time or the place, and yet I couldn't help but rise to meet the challenge he was giving me. "No, Agent Phillips, I hardly think the five minutes we spoke counts as 'keeping company.'"

"I'll have to make sure I practice that while I'm here, then." He grinned at me before looking around at the others. "Maybe these guys can teach me their secrets." Then he raised his glass. "Regardless, congratulations."

"Yes," Grace added, and then we all joined in, lifting our glasses and toasting to the happy couple. I smiled too, unable to shake the feeling that I'd fought a battle and lost, but at the same time, feeling like I wanted to dive back into the fight again.

"I'll be right back," Daniel said, brushing a kiss across Emma's cheek and disappearing out the front door.

"Are we having it at our place?" Grace asked, getting back to the topic at hand and not the business of honeymoons.

"I don't know yet," Lena said. "I know the weather can be unpredictable, but I've always wanted to get married outside. The nice thing about having so many of the wedding things under your own control is having the flexibility. We'll have to have a girls' day and talk about it."

Kate laughed and leaned into Noah. "I'm all for that. I need a break."

"Me too," I agreed.

Cole looked at me like clockwork, gaze skimming over me before he raised an eyebrow, like he was asking me exactly what kind of break I needed and if he was going to be involved in it.

"Fuck," I muttered under my breath.

Lena picked up the wine bottle and looked in it. "Oops, looks like we need more. Come on, Rayne."

"I'm okay."

She grabbed me by the arm and pulled me up, tugging me over to the bar by the fireplace, and I let her. "Girl, what is going on?"

"I don't know what you're talking about."

Lena rolled her eyes and actually looked through the bottles of wine. "Like hell, Rayne. You and I know each other better than that."

"He gets under my skin so fast," I whispered. "And he *loves* that he's doing it. I just need him to go away."

"You know who this reminds me of?"

"Who?"

She glanced behind her. "Grace and Harlan. I know you weren't as close with all of us back then, but they were at each other's throats constantly. And now…"

There was no need to finish the sentence. I knew.

Over the years, some of these people had been my clients. But as we grew closer as friends and a community, I had to step back as their therapist. Now I only worked with clients of the ranch itself. Ethically, I couldn't do anything else.

"This isn't the same," I said.

"No?"

"It's *not*."

She held up her hands. "Fair enough. But I'm just saying… No one will deny I'm the town expert on knowing when a man looks at you and wants you. I did it for three years. And that man?" Her voice dropped to a whisper. "That man wants you so badly, the whole room knows it."

"Well, I don't want him."

"All of us know that's a lie," Evie said, reaching between us and taking the bottle of wine Lena still held hostage.

I sighed, glancing back at the table. Our absence was conspicuous. "Not now, Evie."

"All right," she said mildly. "But it better be soon."

A laugh finally came out of me. "Fine."

Thankfully, dinner went back to normal.

Mostly.

I was still aware of every move Cole made, and I found his eyes on me more than once. But I tried—and failed—to ignore it. The undercurrent of energy that made me want to push him and fight with him just so he fought back was strong.

What was wrong with me?

For the most part, no one bothered me or commented on my being quiet. All the women in the room already knew why —and most of the men too.

Finally, when dinner was over and I'd done my part to help clean, I waved goodbye. Cole was still here, but I thought I could slip out before we had another awkward or charged moment.

"You better come by Deja Brew," Evie said as I put on my coat. "I'm serious."

"I will."

Now I knew why Cole chose Montana Jewels as the meeting spot.

I settled into my car with a sigh. And…nothing. The key

41

was turned in the ignition, but there was no sound at all. Not even a hint of the engine turning over.

"You have got to be kidding me," I said.

Desperation took over, and I kept trying to get the engine to start unsuccessfully. I slumped over and leaned my head on the steering wheel, defeated.

"Shit."

## Chapter 7

**Cole**

THE WAY RAYNE slumped over in the seat of her car made me wince. I didn't like seeing her in distress. However, and it might make me a bad person, I was glad her car had died. Simply because it gave me another chance to talk to her. She'd avoided me for the rest of the night after our little back-and-forth about Chicago.

I liked that I riled her up. Something about the way she flushed and glared at me made me want to do it again and again.

Maybe it was because Rayne Westerfield was holding everything back. I could see it. *Feel* it. Always cool, always professional, until someone got under her skin enough for her to let go. And I liked being the one who made her crack the measured, even exterior.

It made me remember the one true time I saw her let go and how fucking beautiful it was. What would I have to do to see that side of her again without crossing any lines? Because I felt something between us, and every action and move she made told me she felt it too.

Approaching the door of the car, I didn't want to scare her. "Car trouble?"

She jerked up from where she leaned on the steering wheel, focusing on me through the window. "Unfortunately."

It was already dark, and it was cold. She pushed open the door, and I stepped back to let her. "I'll have to see what the problem is."

"Why don't you let me drive you home?" I asked. "It's late, it's cold, and you're not going to figure it out tonight. Even if you did, there's probably not a garage open right now."

The look on her face told me she knew I was right, but she also didn't want to admit it. She was going to tell me no, and that was fine. I expected it. I had a few months to show her I wasn't the man she thought I was.

Rayne opened her mouth to refuse—it was written all over her face—and the door behind us opened, followed by laughter. Grant and Cori came out of the lodge, firmly wrapped in each other's arms.

He lifted her up and tossed her over his shoulder as she squealed. "Grant, what are you doing?"

"I'm taking my wife home," he said, matter-of-fact.

"Put me down." She was still laughing.

He made a sound of consideration as he carried her down the steps. "No, I think I like you right here." As they passed, he waved to both of us, and Cori looked up through her hair. "Bye, Rayne, Cole!"

"Bye," Rayne said. She watched them with the same longing with which she watched Jude and Lena during dinner. Did other people find her as easy to read as I did? Or was it just me?

"All right," she said quietly and sighed. "I'll be able to get it tomorrow, and I don't want to bother anyone with better things to do."

I ignored the subtle dig at me because I didn't want to have anything better to do than be with her. I also did the selfish thing and didn't suggest we try to jump her car, because I wanted to spend some time with her, and this was an innocent way to do it.

Gesturing toward my truck, I stepped back. "After you."

Rayne grabbed her bag from the car and went straight to the correct truck. So, she had been paying attention when I left Montana Jewels the other day. Good to know.

I opened the door for her and resisted the urge to help her up. "Thank you," she said before I closed it.

"It's not a problem, Rayne." Walking around, I swung up into the driver's seat. "Which direction am I going?"

"I'm on the other side of town."

The nicer side, if I was remembering the full layout of Garnet Bend correctly. It would take me some time to memorize everything.

We settled into a quiet, but it was a comfortable quiet. In spite of the tension at dinner and the chemistry that sang between us, there was no awkwardness in the air. Just peaceful silence and the sound of my engine.

"What the hell are you really doing here, Cole?" she finally asked, pointing where to turn off the main road. "Of all the places in the world, you chose here?"

A few more turns, and we pulled up to a nice little house with a good amount of property around it. When I hopped out of the truck, she waited for me to jog around and open the door. This time, I did take her hand and help her down.

"It's as good as any other place."

"That's not a reason."

I sighed. "Because Daniel came to visit me in the hospital when no one else did. And the people here are some of the only people who know me and can still look me in the eye, even after I was the king of all jackasses.

"So when Daniel had a lead on this place, it felt like…it felt like it was meant to happen. It was a good time to come here and let the FBI figure out what they want to do with me and for me to figure out what I want for myself."

We were at her door now, and she fiddled with her keys.

"But Rayne, I'm not going to pretend it had nothing to do with you."

Her breath caught. "Cole—"

"Let me finish," I said gently. "There is something between us, and I know you feel it. I know you're scared of it. And I'm not going to pressure you into something you don't want. But I will be here for the next four months, and I want to show you who I am. Who I can be. I'm the man who's going to challenge you and make you blush and tease you, because I don't think you have anyone in your life who does that. But if, when I leave, you still don't want whatever this is? I promise you'll never hear from me again."

She turned toward me. "You could have gone anywhere."

"But I came here."

The way she looked up at me, she wasn't trying to move away. She was leaning closer. "You drive me a little crazy."

I couldn't stop the smile on my face. "I know."

We came together like an explosion.

Her lips felt just as soft under mine as they had the first time, when we'd been pressed up against my car. Now I couldn't help but press her up against her door. Because I needed more of her. *More* of her, and I needed to feel every inch of her against me.

No whiskey this time, just that damn cherry lip gloss flavor that haunted my dreams and had me waking up, panting, hard and aching for this incredibly beautiful, fucking *maddening* woman.

Rayne wound her hands around my neck, and my fingers were in her hair, holding her steady. Drawing her deeper into me. I pulled her away from the door and molded her body to mine, one arm keeping her close, because something deep and raw was satisfied when I held her. And no matter how long I kissed her, I couldn't escape the feeling that it wouldn't be enough.

She groaned and pressed her hands to my chest, pushing me away. Letting her go was the hardest thing I'd ever had to do.

"I can't," she breathed.

Her words were a knife in my gut. Just like the first time. They were laced with emotion I couldn't interpret, but it didn't seem like she wanted them to be true either.

"Rayne—"

"I'm sorry." Her voice was small and quiet. "I'm sorry, Cole. I can't."

Like she didn't believe the words she was saying, she rose on her toes and kissed me softly one more time before turning and unlocking the door.

She closed it behind her, and I stared at it, unsure of what to do or say. What was there to say? She hadn't pushed me away at first, and she hadn't denied it when I said there was something between us she was afraid of.

There *was* something.

But something else was getting in the way.

I meant what I said. While I lived here, I would challenge her and show her the man I could be. And if it wasn't enough, then it wasn't enough. Pressing a hand to my chest, I ignored the pain of that feeling.

For long moments, I stared at Rayne's door, hoping she would change her mind and come back outside.

She didn't.

Scrubbing a hand over my face, I went back to my truck and started the drive back to the cabin. Rayne said she couldn't. Not that she didn't want to. I would hold on, and be there, in case that *couldn't* turned to *could*.

# Chapter 8

**Rayne**

GOD, why did conferences need to give away so much crap?

I sat on the floor of my living room, the bags and swag from the Chicago conference in a big pile. Absolutely everything, from advertisements for new billing and filing systems, to personal cards of therapy specialists in case we ourselves needed help.

Every therapist should have a therapist, and I did. But I doubted I was going to find a new one in the midst of all the brochures, pens, bags, notebooks and notepads, magnets, and even a flash drive.

I didn't remember which table the flash drive was from, but I put it in the keep pile. More often than not, I found myself needing small gadgets. Might as well keep one for free.

Some of the pens, I kept, and one of the tote bags with less...overt branding. But all the rest I guiltily put into the trash and recycling. Every time I went to a conference, I swore I would just do the culling while I was there. Then I arrived, and

I ended up shoving everything into whatever bag I had with me because the conferences were full of people, and it was easier to just take everything.

I turned on the coffee and the news before I stashed the loot I'd decided to keep in the single tote bag and stuck it in the back of a small closet in my home office, where I probably wouldn't look at it for a few months. Having it out of sight and out of mind was more important than putting it away.

I had enough things on my mind.

Like making sure all my clients were in good shape, and lips on mine that I shouldn't want there.

I turned and went back to the coffee before I could get caught up in the memory of Cole pressing me up against my front door and kissing me the way I'd always dreamed of being kissed.

But I couldn't. No matter how much I wanted to, I couldn't.

As a therapist, I should be able to say the fear I held on to was irrational, and that it shouldn't stand in the way of something I truly wanted. Yet, I had evidence—over and over and over again—of bad things happening to people I cared about.

Hell, anyone in my general vicinity seemed to have a general disposition toward danger. All you had to do was look at Garnet Bend the last few years. Granted, I wasn't arrogant enough to believe all the things that had happened to my group of friends were my fault. But given my own history, it felt personal.

And for my own sanity, I couldn't let any more bad things happen. I had a good life, and I was happy enough. This was something I could live with. The grief of another person in close proximity being hurt?

I couldn't live with that.

No matter if it was irrational, it was my shit to deal with, and I was still in the process of it.

Shaking my head, I grabbed eggs from the fridge and started cooking, listening to the news in the background. The scent of coffee began to permeate the kitchen, the routine of a normal breakfast centering me.

"Now, for a bit of news we don't normally see. It almost seems as if it's out of a movie. After all, we don't talk about the mafia much anymore." The male anchor's voice penetrated my thoughts.

"I agree," the woman took over. "It's definitely not a story you hear every day. The body of a woman was found in the Chicago River over the weekend, and the police have finally released her details. We're told it's a suspected mafia killing in relation to the ongoing trial of Thomas Peretti. While we don't have many details yet, Chicago police and the FBI are asking anyone who might have information about this woman, Susan White, to come forward."

I glanced at the TV quickly and did a double take. The kitchen was warm from my cooking, but my entire body went cold.

It was her.

The woman who ran into me in the hotel lobby. It had been clear she was in distress, but she'd entirely disappeared, and the men following her had been forced to leave. Where had she gone? And how long after I saw her was she killed?

Nausea rose in my stomach. I turned off the eggs and leaned over the sink, afraid I was going to throw up. It could be a coincidence. But given the line of thoughts that had plagued me all morning?

Hell.

All I had were my instincts guiding me, but if anything those anchors said was true about it being mafia-related? I was seen with a murder victim shortly before her death. That wasn't small.

I turned off the coffee and tossed the eggs before grabbing

my purse and following my gut. If any people might know what to do in this situation, it was the guys at Resting Warrior.

Almost everyone at the ranch had been my client at one time or another, but once it became clear the personal lines were blurring, I had gently shifted them away to other professionals I trusted. Not even Mara was with me now. It was better this way since I didn't have to trip over rules of ethics.

Nothing they shared would ever be public, but I was grateful I could go to them as a friend and not a colleague right now.

I called one of the few cabs in town. This would be the perfect time to pick up my car as well. Daniel had texted earlier that they'd been able to get it started, something about a loose cable.

My stomach growled, and I rolled my eyes. There was no way I could eat right now, despite my body's thoughts to the contrary.

Jude was walking up the steps to the lodge when I pulled up. He smiled and started to wave when he saw me getting out of the car. "Is this a social call?"

"No," I managed. "Well, I hope it will turn out that way, but no, not yet."

"What's going on?"

I led the way up the steps and into the lodge and sat in one of the comfy chairs near the empty fireplace.

Jude looked toward the stairs. "Do we need anyone else?"

"I'll take whoever's here," I said. "I hope I'm overreacting, but…"

He held out a hand. "Stay put. I'll be right back."

Jogging up the stairs, he disappeared, and I slumped back in the chair. Was there something else I could have done? Was there a way I could have found her and helped her?

More than Jude came back down. Daniel, Lucas, Liam, and Grant were all with him.

"Sorry we don't have the whole crew," Daniel said. "Noah and Harlan are delivering a horse. But the rest of us were meeting. Good timing."

"It's fine," I said.

"Are you all right?" Daniel sat the closest to me on the nearby couch, and the other guys arrayed themselves around him.

I shook my head. "I'm fine, but I was watching the news this morning. There's been a murder in Chicago."

Jude frowned. "As sad as that is, it's not exactly out of the norm."

"No," I said. "What's out of the norm is that I've seen her. She ran into me—full body and full speed—in the lobby of the conference hotel the night before I left. After I ran into Cole. She was being chased, and I helped the concierge get the men chasing her out, but when I looked, I couldn't find her. Now she's dead."

The silence in the room was deafening.

"Did you speak to her?" Grant asked.

"No. She ran into me and then past me into the hotel. I saw she was being followed, so I took care of that first."

He looked at the others, and that didn't make me feel better. I blew out a breath. "I know it could be a coincidence and might be nothing to do with me at all. But they're saying it's the mafia. What are the odds? And I can't get it out of my head that I was probably one of the last people she had direct contact with before she was killed. What if it gives the people who killed her a connection to me? God, I sound paranoid." I dropped my head into my hands.

"You don't," Jude said, phone in his hand. "I think I speak for everyone when I say we'd rather our friends be paranoid."

Liam nodded. "Agreed. It might be a coincidence, but in case it isn't, we'll check it out."

"Tell us everything you can remember," Lucas said as he leaned against the wall. "The whole thing, all the details."

I did, glossing over my conversation with Cole, and ending with me leaving the hotel and going back to my family's apartment.

"All right," Daniel said. "We'll look into everything. You found it, Jude?"

Steps sounded outside, and the door opened, revealing Cole. My whole body went tight.

"Yeah. It's all over the media. They're clearly trying to get the word out to the whole country just in case, which is an interesting call, but gives a little insight. They must be desperate."

"Or they know more about things than they're putting out in their statements," Daniel said, eyes on mine.

I swallowed, taking a deep breath in and out. Everything would be fine. It was fine.

Liam looked over his shoulder and waved to Cole. "You ready to talk?"

Cole nodded. "Yeah." My eyebrows rose in question, and he answered it before I could even ask, because Cole's eyes had never left mine. "I might be helping out on the ranch while I'm here so I don't lose my mind in solitude."

"Oh."

"What's going on?" he asked, looking at the guys and finally back at me.

Daniel gestured to me. "Rayne can fill you in if she likes. In the meantime, we'll look into it and let you know."

I glanced at my phone. Time to go if I was going to make a stop at Deja Brew to shut my stomach up before getting to the office and ready for my first session of the day. "Thank you. Really."

I walked past Cole, and he followed me outside. "Rayne, are you okay? What's going on?"

"It's nothing. Just me being overly paranoid."

"Maybe I can help."

Despite wanting to turn to him, I didn't. "I don't need saving, Cole." I didn't need the confusion he brought into my head. I didn't need the temptation he represented. I needed to stay clear.

He didn't follow me down the stairs, but he was still standing there watching as I started my car and drove away. I didn't stop at Deja Brew. Tea in my office would have to do. Seeing Lena and having her question things wasn't something I was ready for. But telling them? Having friends who had my back?

All I felt was relief.

I parked my car around the back of my office like I normally did, leaving the curb parking on Main Street for my clients. They had enough to worry about without fighting for parking. My keys jingled, familiar and soothing.

Until I reached for my doorknob, and the door floated open in front of me.

Oh god.

I pushed the door open, and the papers on the floor told me enough. The office was a mess. The front room with all my records and the office itself. Every drawer had been emptied, and every book was off the shelf. My computer was intact, and nothing was broken. At first glance, it looked like nothing was missing.

But at the end of the day, it didn't matter. I was the last person to see a murder victim alive, and now my office was in pieces. Even I had a hard time believing this was a coincidence.

But I would cling to hope until the last possible second.

## Chapter 9

**Cole**

I KNEW BETTER than to ask the guys why Rayne was at the ranch. They wouldn't violate her privacy, nor should they. But I couldn't ignore what I was feeling either. Something was wrong.

My instincts were going crazy. Granted, my instincts hadn't served me well over the last year. But when it came to Rayne? That was a different story.

I followed them into the security office, where Jude was already sitting. My eyes strayed to the screen before I could even think better of it, and I registered the word *Chicago*.

That was all I needed. I might be on leave, but I was still an agent. I had people I could talk to.

"So, we don't have any problems with you helping out," Daniel said, sitting down. "Depending on what needs to happen day-to-day. We're still stalled on the building, but once we're clear, we're happy to have you there. In the meantime, we can train you to work with the animals and anything else that comes up. Especially after the new building opens, we'll need people. But this will be a good test."

I chuckled. "I'll just be happy to get out of the cabin. Wherever you need me is fine. But can I start tomorrow?"

The test was something we'd already talked about. This was an opportunity to see how well I integrated into the culture here and if the rest of the guys could see me closing the gap my run of being an asshole had created. One family dinner was good, but it wasn't enough to heal everything. Nor should it be.

Liam shrugged. "We're not huge on schedules here. As long as everything gets done, we're happy. If there's something that's actually urgent or needs to be on a schedule, we'll let you know."

"Something come up today?" Jude asked, looking at me. His screen was conspicuously blank now.

"Yeah," I said. "Need to make some calls. Not sure how long it will take."

Neither of those statements was a lie.

"Just let us know when you're in," Lucas said. "We'll find you something to do. Even if it's more sparring."

"I won't say no to that," I laughed, waving as I headed to the truck. I was tempted to head home, but the signal wasn't as good up there, and I didn't want to wait. I drove over to Deja Brew and headed inside. Lena smiled at me as she served me coffee, but there was a rush, so we didn't have a chance to chat.

Pulling out my phone, I called one of my only remaining friends in the Seattle field office. He answered right away. "Jared Warwick, Seattle field office."

"Jared, it's Cole Phillips."

I heard the creak of his chair leaning back. "Cole Phillips. Hey, man. Been a bit."

"Yeah."

"Heard they kicked you out of Chicago."

I laughed once. It did feel that way, but I wouldn't let it show. "More like a voluntary leave of absence. Everything will be fine."

"I'm sure. Anyone who thinks you did anything wrong has another think coming. But I'm guessing since you're calling from your *voluntary* exile, you need something."

"Just a curiosity more than anything else. And obviously, I'm not asking for anything classified. Just curious if there's something actually happening in Chicago."

"Other than you getting kicked to the curb?" Jared was teasing, but there was also an edge to his voice.

"Yeah, other than that."

"Why? What do you know?"

I shook my head even though he couldn't see me. "Nothing. Just heard a rumor, was curious if I was missing anything fun."

A long pause stretched on the other end of the line. "Look, Cole, this is serious. If you know anything about what's going on there, I need you to tell me, okay? It's not a joke."

"I'm not joking," I said. "I don't know anything."

And more than anything, it answered my question. His wasn't the reaction you got if everything was business as usual.

I flipped the phone to speaker and opened the web browser, keeping the volume low. "Yeah," Jared said. "You don't strike me as the kind of guy to go poking with nothing in his pocket. Especially with everything that happened."

"Jared, I'm in Montana. I'm going a bit stir-crazy, and it hasn't even been a week. How the hell would I know about anything happening in the Chicago field office while I'm in the middle of nowhere?"

It was my mistake not to Google this before calling him. The stories were everywhere, and it wasn't hard to figure out why. I didn't know why Rayne was connected to Thomas

Peretti, or how, but the brand-new stories about a mafia-related murder in Chicago were the only reason I could think of she would go straight to Resting Warrior. And more, that she would look the way she did. Drawn and nervous.

One of the things I loved about Rayne was how solid she was. She didn't let anything rattle her—or rather, she *tried* not to let anything rattle her. Including me. I knew, too, a vulnerable woman protected beneath the shell.

What I'd seen this morning wasn't vulnerability. It was terror, pure and simple. Rayne was afraid, and that was the last emotion I wanted her to experience.

"Just because you're in Montana doesn't mean your connections are dead. You're calling me, right? You could have called other people."

"Jared." I scrubbed my hand over my face. "I was curious, okay? It's not a secret about the murder. It went public. I was just in Chicago. I don't know anything. I just wanted a little news. I'm dying out here."

Telling him I knew someone who might know something? That wasn't going to happen. Not until I knew what was going on—and why.

Rayne would probably be pissed at me for digging when I shouldn't have been. But she could be pissed at me all she wanted. You didn't play with the fucking mafia. If there was any chance at all—

I slammed a metal door down on those thoughts. Not now. Not while I was on the phone with Jared. Not until I could get a clear head.

Jared sighed. "Sorry, man. It's just… I can't tell you anything, and you already know that. But people are spooked over there. So if, for whatever reason, you end up knowing something? Don't hold it back. It would only be a good thing for you."

"Noted. Thanks for taking the time."

"No problem—and, Phillips?" He paused. "Try not to get lost in the woods, okay? They might not be able to show it, but there're plenty of people here who miss you."

"Thank you," I said. "Take care of yourself."

I hung up and kept scrolling through the stories. The woman—the murder victim—wasn't someone I recognized. Regardless, if this was what Rayne was worried about, I needed to speak with her. Chicago wasn't my home, but I'd been there long enough to know these people were serious, and you didn't mess with them, even by accident.

Lena was still swamped when I left, but she threw me a wave. I was sure Jude would know I was here today. And if Lena told him I'd been on the phone, it would back up my story.

*Stop it.*

I needed to stop acting like I had something to hide. None of the guys at the ranch would care about Rayne and me. Some of them already knew about my interest. These people weren't out to get me, and acting like it wasn't going to endear me to them.

It was a hard habit to break.

Rayne's office was close. If she wasn't in a session, I would see if she was willing to talk to me. I was risking her anger, but perversely, it made me smile. When Rayne was pissed at me, she wasn't pushing me away, and that was only a good thing.

My heart dropped when I saw her office. Yellow police tape crossed over the door with a uniformed officer at the entrance. His car sat on the curb. Pure terror ran through me. Had she gone straight to her office after she left the ranch? In that case, it hadn't been too long.

I put the truck in gear, passing the officer before accelerating. Rayne had my number. I didn't have hers. There was no way for me to call her and ask what was going on, but I needed to know if she was okay. I *needed* to know if she was safe.

I barely slowed down, speeding through the roads to where Rayne's house was, slamming to a stop in front, where more police cars were parked. There was no breath in my chest.

PART of my mind was screaming that I didn't have a right to be here, and I wasn't smiling anymore at the thought of Rayne's anger. All I needed to know was if she was safe. Because this thing between us had barely started to bloom, and already, I knew losing her would destroy me.

# Chapter 10

**Rayne**

"I'M SORRY ABOUT THIS."

I blew out a breath and watched Charlie flip over the cover of his notepad and put it away. "Not like you're the one who vandalized my office, Charlie."

"No, but I'm still sorry."

"Thank you."

"We'll get—" The pounding on my front door interrupted him. Probably one of the ranch crew. Things didn't stay secret in Garnet Bend for long.

I went to the door and opened it, my whole body freezing when I saw Cole leaning against the frame, heaving in breath like he'd been running, eyes wild.

"Cole?"

Stepping aside, I let him in as Charlie approached. I walked outside with the sheriff, pulling the door closed. "Like I was saying, we'll get the techs in there as quickly as possible and everything dusted so you can get things back to normal."

"Thank you, Charlie."

"I'll keep you posted." Then he looked behind me at the door. "You okay here?"

I smiled. "I'll be fine."

He headed to his cruiser, and I noted the haphazard way Cole's truck was parked against the curb. Had he sped to get here? What was going on?

Cole stood in the entryway, looking out the front window. "What are you doing here, Cole?"

"Why are the police here?"

"Just routine checkup about some things."

"Really?" Cole's voice went dark, eyes intense as he stepped toward me. "You're going to play that game with me?"

I shook my head. "What game?"

"Rayne."

Turning, I went to the kitchen. I still hadn't had anything to eat today, and I was cranky. The least I was going to do was make myself a cup of tea before I called the rest of my clients and told them I needed to reschedule.

"I know you'll be pissed at me," Cole said. "But I saw Chicago on Jude's computer. I called the FBI, and they wouldn't tell me shit. But they wanted to know *everything* I knew, which tells me it's not nothing. I saw the stories about the murder. Are you mixed up in this? Because this is serious if you are."

"This isn't your business, Cole. *I* am not your business. Jude and the rest of them are just checking on things to make sure. It was probably nothing."

He still looked like he was about to start running or fighting, body tensed up, eyes alert. "And when I went to your office to see if you were free, and there was police tape on the door? That's nothing?"

I shook my head and took a mug out of the cupboard. Cole wasn't wrong, but neither was I. This wasn't his business.

"Nothing was taken, nothing was broken. The most likely scenario is someone was looking for valuables and chose poorly since my office is a refurbished house."

I felt Cole close the distance to me, but I didn't turn around, pulling down my favorite box of tea bags and retrieving one. "Would you like a cup of tea?"

"Do you have a computer in your office, Rayne?"

"Of course I do."

"If someone was randomly looking for something valuable, why didn't they take the computer?"

Finally, I sighed and turned around. He was so close, and everything in my body rejoiced. I didn't look up at him—that was a dangerous game. "I don't know, Cole. Maybe they were looking for jewelry. Who knows? But I'm fine. You didn't have to come all the way over here."

The silence between us lasted so long, I thought he'd turned to stone. When I finally looked up, his gaze was raw. "*Are* you okay?" His words were soft and fervent.

"Why wouldn't I be?"

Anger sparked in his eyes, but not at me. If there was one thing I knew about Cole Phillips, it was that he wouldn't hurt me. "Because I might not be *from* Chicago, but I've been there for the last year. And when I was younger, I did some stints there. I know exactly how ruthless Chicago can be. The mafia is no joke. You have no *fucking* idea the lengths these people will go to tie up loose ends. So please, Rayne, tell me what happened. You might be fine now, but it could change in a fraction of a second."

I blew out a long, slow breath. "If you promise not to relay anything to the FBI, because I'm not ready to do that."

"The Bureau and I aren't exactly on good terms right now."

"That's not a promise and you know it. Don't play word games with me, Agent Phillips. It won't work."

Cole turned away and ran a hand through his hair. "I promise. Fuck, Rayne. I'm not here for the Bureau. I'm here for you."

"Right after I left you at the bar, that woman ran into me. She nearly knocked me over. I helped the hotel staff get the men who were chasing her out of the hotel by pointing them out, and when I went looking for her, she was nowhere. I can't stop thinking about her and if she's okay. That's all that happened. It's *nothing*, and I'm being paranoid even asking them to look into things for me."

"You and I both know that's not true." Cole invaded my space again. I pressed myself up against the counter in a failed attempt not to feel the heat coming off him. Everything was mixed up in my mind. The terror of possibly being involved with a crime that could follow me here. The fear of Cole getting hurt—even through this situation—by letting him too close. The desire to grab his shirt, haul his body against mine, and let him finish what he started the other night. All of it was a vortex inside me, and I couldn't breathe.

"You need to leave," I said.

"Rayne, this is serious."

I glared at him. "You think I don't fucking know? This is my office and my life. I know it's serious."

"Then *act like it*."

Cole's face was a mask of fury, but even anger couldn't hide the desire there too. It would be so easy to lean forward and kiss him. And give in. But I couldn't.

I gripped the edge of the counter so hard, I was shaking in an attempt not to move.

Neither of us spoke, and in the silence, my determination was crumbling. I needed to open my mouth and tell him to leave. He couldn't be near me, especially now.

*Come on, Rayne. Get it together.*

A knock on the door broke us apart, and I was relieved I

wasn't the only one who seemed unsettled. The knock came again, but it wasn't the insistent, blazing knock Cole had used when he'd arrived.

Taking a deep breath, I closed my eyes. I needed to be firm, even if it hurt him. Otherwise, he would keep trying, and I would give in. That couldn't happen, because I'd rather push him away now than weather whatever the universe would throw at us once I did. "I appreciate your concern, Cole. But as I said, I'm not yours to take care of, and you're sticking your nose where it doesn't belong. So please go."

He blew out a breath, and I saw the refusal on his lips before he could even speak. "Get the hell *out, Cole*."

"Fine," he said, voice low. "I'm going. But I need you to understand this, Rayne. I'm here. You might not want my help, and that's fine. But if you *need* my help? I don't care if you think you're not my business, I'll come if you call. You know how to get ahold of me."

The knock at the door came again, and I followed him back into the entryway and watched him throw open the door and pass a very shocked Lena and Grace, standing there with a plate of cookies.

"Ladies," he said quietly, but he didn't stop.

All three of us watched him as he got into his truck and drove away, but not before he gave me the most scorching look in the history of the world. I wasn't sure if it was a look of hatred or desire.

Maybe both.

"What the hell was that?" Grace asked.

"A man trying to insert himself where he has no business being."

Lena smirked and pushed past me into the house. "Based on chemistry alone, I think you should let him *insert* himself anywhere he wants to."

"Oh my god, Lena."

She shrugged, grinning unapologetically as she set the cookies down on the kitchen counter. "I'm just saying. I watched this one—" she pointed to Grace "—and Harlan verbally beat the shit out of each other forever, and now they're so in love it's disgusting."

Grace laughed. "Be careful, Lena. Because you and Jude are definitely giving us a run for our money."

"Do you guys want tea?"

"Tea would be great." Lena sat at the breakfast bar. "But are you okay? That's actually why we're here. Not to tease you about Cole. We heard about the break-in."

I added more water to the kettle. "I figured. Actually, when Cole barged in here, I thought it was one of you guys. News travels fast."

"How are you feeling?" Grace asked. "Break-ins are scary."

Turning away, I grabbed more mugs from the cupboard and weighed the wisdom of what to tell them. The guys wouldn't betray my privacy, but it *was* unnerving, and I needed to talk it out. "Okay," I said. "I'm feeling okay about the break-in, but it's everything else. You guys have some time?"

"Absolutely," Lena said. "Spill."

We let the water continue to heat, and I spilled.

# Chapter 11

**Rayne**

WHENEVER YOU'RE FREE, *come over to the lodge*.

Jude's text made me feel a mixture of relief and nerves. I knew all of them well enough to know they wouldn't communicate anything regarding a sensitive situation over any channel that could be monitored. Even good news.

*Will do.*

Outside the window, snow fell. Early this year. It was always a gamble whether we would get the first snow before Halloween. This year? Clearly.

Even if we got snow, it wasn't normally this heavy this early. But already, the news was reporting a big storm coming in. I needed to grab some extra food and essentials from the store on the way back from the ranch, just in case.

Because my office was still a crime scene, I took my clients' video calls in the kitchen. I missed the intimacy and energy of the sessions in the office, but it was certainly cozier. I kept sweatpants on and made myself hot chocolate. It felt appropriate for the snow outside.

When I finally ended my last call, I looked outside and deflated. I needed to get over to the ranch before the snow got too bad. The last thing I needed was to be stuck in a ditch and have to be rescued.

Thankfully, the plows around Garnet Bend did a good job, and the roads were still clear. And doubly thankfully, despite his saying he would work for the ranch, I didn't see Cole's borrowed truck. So there was no chance of us having a repeat of yesterday.

But when I walked into the security office, Jude and Daniel looked grim. "Why does it feel like I just walked into a funeral?"

"Sit down," Daniel said. "It's not the worst…"

"But it's not good," Jude finished, typing on the computer. Multiple monitors were set up, and a second later, a video spread across all of them. It wasn't hard to recognize. This was the hotel lobby in Chicago. There I was, and there was Cole, talking to me.

On the screen, I stepped away, and not even a minute later, the woman crashed into me. The rest of the scene was exactly what I remembered. I could be seen going to the desk and pointing out the men. The cameras even caught me venturing farther into the hotel to look for the woman.

"Can I see the beginning again?"

We watched her crash into me once more, this time slower. Her hand went into my bag and came back out. I didn't remember that part, but nothing had been missing when I'd gone through it. Probably just because of the way she ran into me and tried to keep her balance.

"You're looking at her hand?" Jude asked.

"Yeah. Nothing was missing from my bag. It looks intentional, but it could be a coincidence."

Daniel chuckled. "A lot of coincidences right now. Your office?"

I shook my head. "I don't know what I'm supposed to say. I'm on camera with this woman. Clear as a bell. But no one's tracked me down to ask me about her. If the authorities haven't…"

The look on Jude's face told me everything.

"Do you think I'm in danger?" I asked. "Honestly."

"Honestly? I don't know. I think it's convenient she was announced as a murder victim and then your office was broken in to. But on the surface, there's absolutely nothing to connect you to this woman. That doesn't mean you're out of the woods, but it's clear you didn't even speak to her. With the exception of her hand going into your bag, there's no reason to think you had anything to do with her or her murder."

I rubbed my temples. "Yeah. So, I'm okay to go home?"

"You have an alarm system?" Daniel asked.

"Yes." There wasn't anyone in the Resting Warrior family who didn't. It's the way it was. They would show up and install one if they had to. "And bear spray."

"And an escape plan?"

That was less firm. I did have ways out of the house, but I hoped I wouldn't have to use them. "Yeah, I'll be okay."

Daniel looked like he was considering sending someone to sit outside my house. "It's freezing," I said. "And it's only going to get worse if what they say about the storm is true. Don't any of you dare spend the night in your car to watch me."

"We could sleep on the couch." Jude smirked.

"Do you really think it's necessary?"

He sighed. "It's hard, because I think all of us would rather err on the side of caution. Always. But because we don't have any proof of anything beyond a weird coincidence, it's more about how you feel, Rayne. If you feel unsafe, we will make sure you are. If you feel safe, then we'll keep tabs from a distance."

I thought about it. Did I feel safe?

Yes.

I did. Last night, I hadn't felt even a shiver of fear, nor all of today when I was doing my client appointments in the kitchen. The alarm system they'd helped install was one of the best on the market, and I did sleep with bear spray next to the bed.

"I think I feel okay," I said. "But thank you."

"You know you can call us if that changes," Daniel said.

I nodded. "Thank you. I should get back before the snow gets too bad."

"Keep us posted, please."

"I will."

All I wanted was to get back home, but I did stop for a few things at the store, and it was already getting dark. I wasn't afraid in my home, and the alarm system made me feel even better.

Everything would be fine.

A LOUD THUMP WOKE ME.

I jerked awake, looking around my dim bedroom. There was a touch of ambient light due to the snow, the way the moon reflected off the white, making the night fully visible.

What had woken me?

A creak downstairs had my blood running cold. That creak was the floorboard between the kitchen and the living room. A distinctive whine I'd grown used to over the years.

*Someone was in my house.*

I glanced at the bedside clock. The face was dark and empty. No power. Shit. Moving as quickly and quietly as I could, I got out of bed, and moving on instinct, I pulled the covers up to make it look like I'd never been in the bed.

Now would be a great time to use that escape plan, but there wasn't any way to move in this house without noise. It was older and creaky, and it was still snowing. If they didn't think I was here—maybe I went somewhere in someone else's car—I had a better chance. I didn't know where the instinct came from, but the Resting Warrior guys always talked about the power of instincts, so I was going to follow them.

Another creak came from downstairs.

I smoothed down the pillows and made it look perfect before I grabbed the bear spray and my phone and crawled under the bed.

*Real smart, Rayne.*

The movie *Taken* came to mind, where they found her under the bed and kidnapped her. But the kidnappers had known she was in the house and where to look. I tried to slow my breathing.

From down the hall, I heard the sounds of someone climbing the stairs. I knew the sequence of noises by heart. It seemed like just one person, but I didn't know for sure.

Step by heavy step, they came closer. Whoever it was wasn't bothering to hide their presence.

The door to my room pushed open silently. I should have called nine-one-one, but they might have been able to hear the dispatcher and give me away. A set of black boots stood in the doorway. They stood there for long moments, just looking.

Stepping inside, they suddenly moved quickly. My closet opened, and I heard the sounds of clothes being thrown on the floor. He turned out my drawers before leaving the room and striding through the house like he owned it.

Within a minute, sounds of crashing and shuffling came from downstairs in my office. He was looking for something, and seemed not to think I was here. That was good. That was *really* good.

I'd wanted to believe the incident at my other office was a coincidence. Now, I couldn't. My heart pounded in my throat, adrenaline and terror still singing through my veins. I wasn't safe yet.

They moved on, tearing apart my house with systematic precision. I was grateful that, for the most part, I was a minimalist. I didn't have a lot of things to go through here.

It seemed like forever before I heard him leave. And shortly after, the heat came on, and one glance out from beneath the bed showed me a blinking clock. He was gone. I crawled out from beneath the bed and leaned against it, still unwilling to get off the floor.

My hands shook as I unlocked my phone. I needed to call the police. Daniel and Jude. But my body didn't obey those thoughts. It pulled up Cole's contact and dialed, his words about help the only thing ringing in my mind.

He was the last person I should be calling.

The line only rang once.

## Chapter 12

**Cole**

"RAYNE?" I asked. That was the only person it could be, despite the unknown number. It was three in the morning, and fear struck me straight in the middle of the chest. If Rayne was calling this late, it was serious.

"Cole." Her voice was small. Scared. I was on my feet and pulling on my jeans the second that tone met my eardrums. "I shouldn't be calling you."

"What happened?"

"There was someone in my house."

"*What?*"

Her breath shook as I put her on speaker and pulled on a shirt and my socks. Shoes. I needed shoes. And a coat. Fuck, it was snowing.

"He's gone now. I made the bed so it looked like I wasn't here, and he bought it."

My shoes were on, and I grabbed my keys. "I'm on my way."

"It's okay," she said. "I'll call the police and Daniel. You don't have to come all the way here."

"Like hell," I ground out the words, placing the phone on the seat of the truck beside me. "You call the cops, and then call me back, okay?"

"Okay."

The line went dead, and I focused on getting down the mountain without killing myself. Because I was going to go as fast as humanly possible in this shitty weather. A bit out of season for this kind of storm, but it was northern Montana. What the hell did I know?

I pulled onto the highway as my phone rang. I set it straight to speaker. "You okay?"

"They're on their way."

"Good."

We sat in silence as I drove. Rayne breathed, and I listened to her do it. Before tonight, I don't know if I would have said that I craved the sound of someone's breath, but tonight, I did. Because if she was breathing, she was alive.

"Almost there."

"Charlie's here," she said, palpable relief in her voice.

My hands unclenched on the steering wheel just a little. "Go. I'll be there in a minute."

"Okay."

Her side of the call ended, and I focused on the road ahead of me. I was halfway through town and getting close to her neighborhood. The snow had built up a little since the last plows had gone through, but it was bearable.

The snow whipped past my headlights as I turned into her neighborhood. I already saw the police lights flashing. This time, I parked more carefully by her curb before I went inside.

No knocking. The door was unlocked, and I pushed it open. Charlie, the police chief, noted me, but when Rayne saw me and waved, he stood down.

There were other officers in the house, looking through things. Whatever they could. Because her belongings were everywhere. Drawers turned out and shelves emptied. Nothing was broken or ripped into. Just a frantic, if thorough, search. Was this what her office had looked like?

And Rayne looked…wrecked.

Tired and afraid.

Seeing her whole and safe satisfied something deep inside me, and yet I wanted more. All I wanted was to pull her into my arms and hold her. Make her *feel* safe. But I couldn't do that in front of the officers. Hell, I didn't know if Rayne wanted me to do it at all.

She'd called me, and I was so grateful, but now that I was here, I wasn't sure what she wanted from me. Regardless, whatever she needed, I would do.

Now that she was in my line of sight and safe, I took a breath. The way my stomach had hollowed out at the fear in her voice had been so fucking familiar. But she was here. She was safe. She wasn't Jamie.

"Do you have someplace to go?" Charlie asked.

"Umm…"

I stepped forward. "Yes. Resting Warrior will take her."

Rayne's eyes flickered to mine for a second, and she nodded.

Charlie looked between the two of us. "Hold tight here for a second. I'll have them clear your bedroom so you can grab some things. Doesn't look like that's where his focus was anyway."

"Okay, thanks."

She was in thin pajamas. Pants and a shirt. So different from what I normally saw her in, and I loved the softness it brought to her. But I hated the way her arms wrapped around herself like she was in pain.

"Rayne," I said.

When she looked up, it was like she'd forgotten I was there. That was common in the aftermath of something like this. Adrenaline, shock, all the bodily responses. She wasn't focused. "Hi."

"Can you talk to me for a second?"

She nodded, even going so far as letting me pull her over to the wall and lean her against it so she had some support. Everything in me ached to touch her, and I held back.

"What really happened in Chicago?"

Rayne's eyes locked on mine, and for the first time, I saw true fear there. "I told you. Right after I stopped talking to you, a woman ran into me. But I didn't tell you she was the woman who was murdered."

"Fuck, Rayne."

"I helped point out the men who were following her, and then I left. Jude found the security footage, and that's all it is. But I'm on camera. With her. Her hand went into my bag for a second, but for all I know, it was from her tripping, because nothing was missing. Now this is happening, and I—"

Something ticked in my brain. I touched her shoulder. "Was there anything extra? You checked everything?"

"Yeah. I always do. It's all junk, and I threw most of it away. All of it was branded, except…"

She trailed off and looked away, lost in thought.

"Except for what?"

"Except for the flash drive. An unmarked flash drive. I thought it was one of those things I just picked up and didn't notice. Didn't throw it away because they can come in handy."

I blew out a breath. "It could be nothing. But you still have it?"

"Yeah. If he didn't find it. I'll grab it when I get my clothes."

"Where did you hide?" I asked quietly.

Rayne's cheeks turned pink with shame, and I would do

anything in the world to wipe that look off her face. "Under the bed."

"And he was in the room with you."

Her whole body shook. "Yes. I don't know why he didn't look under the bed, and I don't know how he got past the alarms. But I'm just…relieved. I should have taken them up on their offer to watch."

"Daniel?"

She nodded.

"Hold on a second. I want to see something." I stepped over to the alarm panel by the front door and took off the front. The backup battery was still in place. "Rayne, does your security system use Wi-Fi?"

"Yes."

I replaced the cover of the panel. "After this is over, we'll get you one that doesn't use it."

"It's supposed to be one of the best."

Glancing at the brand, I nodded. "It is. Against a burglar or someone who's trying to steal valuables from you. Not if you're going up against the mob, which has highly motivated people looking for something specific. Your battery is still working, so I'm guessing someone hacked it. We can have Jude confirm."

She shook her head. "All I did was stand in a lobby. How is this happening? I just—"

"Okay, Rayne," Charlie said. "You're free to grab some things. I promise we'll get this processed as fast as possible."

"Thank you."

I looked at her. "Do you want me to come with you or stay here?"

"Stay here. I'll be right back."

She went up the stairs, and even from here, it was easy to see the slump of defeat in her shoulders.

"Been a while," Charlie said to me. "Didn't think I'd ever see you back in this town until yesterday."

I grimaced. "I know. And I apologize for the way me and…" A pause. What the hell did I call him now? "My former partner acted. I hope while I'm here I can show everyone I'm not that person."

His eyebrows rose in surprise. "It might take some time. We small-town folk have long memories. But we'll give you a shot."

"I appreciate that."

Pulling out my phone, I dialed Daniel. It took a few rings, but he answered sleepily. "Phillips?"

"Rayne's house was broken in to. She's okay, but her house is trashed. We'll be coming there soon. There's new information about the situation."

"*You're* the one bringing her?"

The question in his tone was warranted. "I am. She called me, and I didn't question it."

Through the phone, I heard him getting up. "What's the new information?"

"Better in person."

"Got it. We'll meet you at the security office."

I hung up. Rayne came down the stairs a few minutes later, heading into her office. "You're taking care of her?" Charlie asked.

I looked at him. "I'm doing my best."

"Keep going," he said with a chuckle.

"I will." It wasn't just a promise. More of a vow.

Rayne emerged from her office and set the small suitcase she carried down by her feet. "Okay."

"Coat?"

She went to the closet and got her coat and pulled on boots. Following behind her, I grabbed a hat off a hook and pulled it down onto her head when she turned around.

"What are you doing?" She gave me a flicker of a smile.

"It's cold out there. Need to keep you warm."

She smiled again, but this time, there was no emotion behind her eyes.

"Let's go."

Charlie waved to the two of us. "We'll get this straightened out, Rayne."

"Thank you."

I picked up her suitcase and closed the door behind us. "Does Charlie know what's really going on?"

"No," she said. "How do I say that the Chicago mafia broke in to my home and office? I'd rather Daniel tell him."

"Fair enough."

Her suitcase was nestled on the floor of the bench seat, and I helped her up into the truck. Before I closed the door, she spoke. "Cole."

"Yeah?"

"Thank you for coming."

# Chapter 13

**Rayne**

"I'M SORRY TO WAKE YOU," I said when Lucas came into the security office, the last one to arrive. Jude and Daniel were already here, and Daniel glared at me.

"It's not a problem, Rayne. Don't worry about that, please."

Cole leaned against the wall, observing everything. He'd been steady and calm since he arrived at the house, never pushing, always making sure I was okay. It was comforting, even though I still wasn't sure why he was the first person I'd called.

"Cole mentioned new information?"

"Yeah." My throat scraped on the word, and I fished the flash drive out of my pocket and placed it on the table. "That was in my bag when I came back from Chicago. I didn't think anything of it. I've gotten flash drives as swag before. But Cole made me think of it. I kept saying nothing was missing from my bag."

"But maybe she left something instead," Jude finished.

"Exactly."

He held out his hand. "You haven't opened it?"

"No."

"Okay, then," he said. "We'll cross our fingers that it's blank and all of this is a misunderstanding."

No one in the room laughed or even smiled. Because we all knew there were too many coincidences for it to be blank. Or nothing. But I hoped all the same.

Jude uncapped the drive and plugged it in. "Encrypted," he said, when a password box opened.

"Can you manage?" Daniel asked.

Jude shrugged. "Yeah, shouldn't be a problem." His fingers flew across the keys, windows popping up. I had no idea what he was doing or the full process of hacking into something encrypted, but I was grateful he had the skills.

"The intruder hacked her security system," Cole said. "I checked the backup battery. It was still there."

Lucas frowned and looked at me. "He cut the power?"

"Yeah." I filled them in on the whole ordeal, watching each one grow more tense the longer I spoke. I knew I was lucky he hadn't found me, but sitting here right now, I didn't feel lucky.

"Got it," Jude said.

It took a few seconds for it to open, but the window on the screen had folders. Lots of them. A whole screen's worth of folders arrayed everywhere.

"I guess it's not blank," I said.

"No."

Jude clicked on one, and the screen populated with pictures. Daniel swore, and I had to look away. Blood appeared on the screen. Not just blood, but someone bloodied. Clearly dead. Head smashed on the concrete beneath them and completely unrecognizable.

"Shit," Lucas said. "That… Please tell me every folder on there isn't a murder."

I waited for the answer, looking at the wall.

"Yeah," Jude said. His voice was raw. "It is. And not just pictures. There are video files as well."

Cole pushed off the wall. "How many?"

"Sixty-two. No guarantee there's only one person per file."

I stood, unable to keep myself still. I needed to move because I felt like I couldn't *breathe*. "Why would they keep these? Of all the things? That mob boss, Thomas Peretti, is on trial. Why would they keep evidence that could put him away for more than one lifetime?"

"There are lots of reasons," Cole said quietly. "The main one being blackmail. Peretti might be the mastermind behind all these killings, but I doubt he did them all personally. They could use this evidence to keep lieutenants in line. Or as a threat there's more to come."

Jude turned in his chair to face us, and thankfully, he didn't leave any pictures open on the screen. "It also explains the encryption."

"How did she get it? That woman. The one who ran into me?"

"Susan White," Jude answered. "She was a reporter. I have no idea how she got her hands on this, but it was a brave fucking thing to do."

I ran both hands through my hair, aware I probably looked like a drowned rat after being under the bed and out in the snow. "Why did they kill her?" I asked. "She didn't have it anymore. She passed it on to me." Logically, I knew why, but I had to verbalize the question.

"If they knew she had it, she already knew too much," Lucas said.

"I think that's why whoever was in your house didn't look very hard for you," Cole added. "You mentioned the security footage. I guarantee they've seen it too and know her hand went into your bag. But it doesn't look like you're aware, right?"

"No." I shook my head. "I looked...startled, I guess."

Cole leaned forward on the table. "What I'm about to say goes against our instincts, but the mafia, for all their reputation, don't kill for fun. They kill for a purpose. If it's clear you have the flash drive but are an innocent bystander, they want to retrieve it. Not to murder someone without a point.

"There's a reason they didn't identify themselves or attack you and make you tell them where the drive is. There's a reason they didn't look in the places where you put something if you're intentionally trying to hide it. None of your cushions were torn. No pictures moved for safes. He didn't look under the bed." His eyes met mine intentionally. "Because they don't think you know what you have."

"I know now," I breathed.

"There's no reason they have to be made aware of that," Daniel said. "We can get this back to them—or to the authorities."

I wrapped my arms around myself, trying to resist the shudder that racked my body. "I *want* to give it to the authorities, because anyone who's done these kinds of things deserves to rot in prison for the rest of their life. But if I do that, they'll keep coming, right?"

No one spoke for a moment, and when I looked up, the men were looking at one another, like they could communicate without words. "What?"

"It's tricky at this point," Cole said. "Because as of this moment, there are a couple of paths. They either think you don't have it, and it's over. Or, they still think you have it, but that you don't know what you have. If you give it back to them, you're telling them you know what's on it. Because in order for you to know who to give it back to, you need to know what's on it."

And my knowing what was on it put my life in danger. It put *all* our lives in danger. If they found out we all knew about it, they would come after everyone to clean up the mess. Daniel and Lucas were fathers now. The *kids*.

Not to mention Susan White, who'd died anyway, even though she tried. What could we do?

"I never should have brought it here," I said. "Now all of you are involved. They'll come after you too."

"We'll be okay, Rayne," Lucas said. "After all this time? We've survived worse."

Jude and Daniel laughed, but there wasn't true humor in it.

I glared at him. "You're a father. You're married. All of you... Our entire...all our friends and family are *here*. And I might bring the people who did *that* right to our doors. If they come here, none of us will be all right."

"For the moment," Daniel said, spreading his hands wide, "we're actually in the best position we could be in. Because they don't have any proof you have this. I want you to stay here for the next few days while we watch anywhere else they could get to you, including your online presence. If they don't touch anything, there's a good chance they think you don't have it. At which point we can anonymously get it to the FBI."

Jude nodded. "I agree."

I felt sick. Everything from the night was catching up to me, and it felt like the tethers that held my world together were detangling faster than the speed of light. Someone had been in my *house*.

God, it seemed silly for that to just be sinking in, but I was standing here, and there were photos of murdered people. For all I knew, I could have been one of them.

My office was in tatters, and so was my home. I knew I could stay here, but with this hanging over my head, dread spiraled through me. As a therapist, I, of all people, knew your reactions were what they were, even if they weren't correct on the first try. Right now, it felt like I was losing everything, no matter that it wasn't the case.

My little suitcase sitting by the door, me in my pajamas and coat. Panic—true fear and panic welled up in my chest. I couldn't do anything to stop it, and right at this moment, the only thing I could do was look at Cole.

And he was looking right back at me.

## Chapter 14

**Cole**

I'D KNOWN something was wrong when I'd left Rayne in her kitchen. I should have pressed her harder right then to tell me the truth. Maybe we could have prevented the look on her face right now.

This was different from when I'd walked into her house tonight. Exhaustion wasn't the emotion on her face. Terror and panic were. She fought it because that was who she was, and she was stronger than most people I knew. But even the strongest people would feel something when faced with being murdered for something they had no involvement with.

She looked at *me*.

There were four men in the room, and the one she looked at when the panic rose was me. Pride and relief swelled in my chest, along with the same desire to pull her close and protect her from the world.

I would protect her now, even if she wasn't aware of it.

The option not to had disappeared when I heard her voice on the phone.

Opening my mouth to ask what she needed, I was interrupted by beeping. Loud, obnoxious beeping coming from the computer.

Jude swore and began typing. Only a few seconds later, he tore the flash drive out of the tower and stood, bending around the array of monitors and pulling the plug. The entire display went dark, and the rest of us stared at him in shock. Pulling the plug on the system like that...

"What the hell just happened?" I asked.

The computers beeped as he plugged things back in and rebooted the computers. No alarms sounded this time, and Jude went back to working as soon as the computers were online. He didn't speak, a muscle in his jaw ticking.

Jude was generally a man of few words—and more than capable. He would tell us when he was ready. But every second that passed grated under my skin. Whatever the hell had happened, it wasn't good.

"Shit," he said under his breath.

"What?"

He looked at me and then turned and looked at Rayne. "I'm sorry, Rayne. There was something on the drive that I missed. A program beneath everything else, designed only to start up after a certain amount of time logged in."

She paled. "What did it do?"

Leaning down, he picked up the little device from where it had landed when he'd pulled it out. "It sent up a flare."

"A *flare?*" Daniel asked.

"Yes. And if I'd let it do its thing, the virus it launched would have eaten through my computer and pretty much destroyed it."

This was bad. Everything we'd told Rayne about her

options was now null and void. Because this changed everything. "Where did it go?" I asked.

"I don't know."

"Any chance you shut it down fast enough that it didn't get
to its destination?"

He wanted to tell me yes; I could see it on his face. But
Jude shook his head. "I don't think so. But if we're lucky, they
only got a wide ping and not an exact location."

I closed my eyes, letting my head fall forward for a second.
Rayne cleared her throat. "Does this mean they know?"

"Yes," I said. "They probably do. Or at least, they know
someone has accessed the flash drive and approximately where."

"We still need to monitor everything to see where we
stand," Daniel said. "That hasn't changed."

"But she can't stay here." I stood up straight. "Now
Rayne's right. Your families need to be protected. And they
know who Rayne is, so they'll know her connection to you. But
if she's not here, you'll be fine. She's the one they want."

Daniel looked at Rayne. All of them did, and in those
looks, I saw how desperately they wanted to help. But this was
beyond what they could do, and they knew just as much as I
did how dangerous it was. We didn't have enough information.
The mafia could be on their way to kill her right now, and we
wouldn't see them coming.

"I'm sorry, Rayne," Lucas said. "I want you to stay."

"No," she said. "I get it. I can barely live with myself,
thinking about Susan White dying when it could have been
prevented. If it were one of you? I couldn't survive it."

Given everything that had happened tonight, I didn't know
how Rayne would take the next words out of my mouth. But
there weren't many options, and I wasn't going to let her stay
at a fucking hotel unless I was staying with her.

"My cabin is off the grid. Not only that, but the owner is a paranoid guy. The basement is a prepper shelter, and I've been instructed very explicitly *not to touch it*." Jude smiled before letting it fall. "Rayne can stay with me until we figure out where everyone stands. The mafia has a location, and we clearly can't send those files to the FBI without taking out their servers. We need to make contact with them quietly."

"That, we can do," Daniel said.

"Thank you. I'm too high on their shit list to make that kind of contact 'quiet,' and they don't trust me enough to take me at my word. But you? Hell, I think they'd bend over backward to make you happy."

Jude took the flash drive and plugged it back into the computer. "Don't worry, I've put protections in place now. This is fine. Just want to check something."

Rayne stared at me. "I can't stay with you."

I met her gaze head on. "Why not?"

"Does this 'off-the-grid' cabin have Wi-Fi? I still have clients I need to see."

"I think your clients would understand missing a session since you're being hunted by the literal mafia, but yes, the cabin has Wi-Fi. But you won't be using it."

She opened her mouth, and I held out a hand. "You want to stay off the grid? You're not online, Rayne. We can use my phone to check in, and the cabin has more than one radio."

"I can drive down to Missoula and stay in a hotel," she said. "Pay in cash."

"Like hell."

Fire blazed in her eyes as she stood. "Are you seriously telling me what I can and cannot do right now?"

Out of the corner of my eye, I saw Jude doing something on the computer, but I said nothing about it. Instead, I focused on the glorious, fiery woman in front of me. For the first time tonight, I'd seen the real Rayne, and I had to fight to keep the smile off my face.

"Yes, Rayne. I am telling you what to do. Because in spite of the fact of making everyone here uncomfortable, I'm still an FBI agent, and I do know a thing or two about protecting people."

"I don't need your help."

Her tone didn't sound that way, but I needed her to do this. "Outside for a second." I gestured out of the security office door.

"Anything you need to say, you can say in front of them."

"Rayne," I sighed. "Please."

She crossed her arms and stormed past me. I gave the others an awkward smile as I followed her out and shut the door.

"Is this the point in the conversation where you lord your status over me again and insist that I need you? Because I'm not dumb, Cole. I might not have experience in fleeing the mob, but I can handle myself."

I pressed the heels of my hands into my eyes. "I never said you couldn't."

"Then why—"

"Why did you call me?" I asked. "Earlier? You could have called the police first or Daniel, Jude, Lucas. Hell, you could have called *Lena* first, but you didn't. You called me."

Rayne stared straight through my chest. "I don't know why."

"Do you trust me?"

Her eyes lifted to mine. "Yes."

"Do you think I'm asking you to come with me under some guise to…I don't know…turn you over to the people who want to hurt you?"

"What? No."

"Then why not?" I dared to take a step closer. "Why not let me help you?"

"I *can't.*"

I stepped forward again and took another risk. Cradling her face in my hands, I made sure she was looking at me. She didn't slap my hands away, and suddenly her breath was short. "You seem to say that a lot around me, but I've never heard a single reason why." Before she could say anything, I forged on. "I'm not asking you to tell me. I'm asking you to let me help you. Even if it's just this once. What I'm not doing is asking you to sell me your soul."

My voice was softer as I resisted the urge to close the distance between us and taste her lips again. Her and that fucking cherry lip gloss. "Just let me help keep you alive. Please."

She searched my face for what felt like an eternity. "Okay."

"Thank you." I relaxed and released her. But I needed to see her spark again, even if it wasn't a smile. "Besides, if you die, how else can I prove that you're missing out on all of this?"

Rayne rolled her eyes when I gestured to my body. "I'm not sleeping with you during this arrangement, just so we're clear."

She stepped back toward the office, and I caught her by the arm. "If you think I'm helping you so you'll owe me some kind of sexual favor, no. I would never force you into anything." I pulled her just a fraction closer. "But if you ask, Rayne, I'll give you *everything*."

"I won't." She pulled her arm from my grip.

*We'll see.*

"Send an email to your clients. You need to shut your phone off before we leave."

Rayne nodded and pulled out her phone. I hadn't seen her computer unless she'd shoved it in the suitcase. She hadn't known she would be going on the run when she'd packed the bag sitting inside the office.

"I hate this," she mumbled, typing out the message and pressing send.

"I know. But your clients will be happier to have you alive."

She couldn't argue with that.

Together, we walked into the office again, and Jude handed Rayne the flash drive. "Everything set?"

I nodded. "Yeah. We'll head up there now."

"With the storm, you might be up there for a few days, no matter what happens. You have everything you need?"

Rayne still stared down at the flash drive in her hands. We needed to keep it with us. Because the only thing worse than the mafia knowing Rayne had it was their knowing—and finding her *without* it. "We could stop by my house and raid the pantry," Rayne said, though her voice was flat.

"No need. I've got supplies for at least a week. Picked them up yesterday." There was no hiding the grin on my face now. For once, the universe was on my side in taking down all the walls Rayne tried to throw up in our way.

Daniel looked at me, and I felt the weight of it. "Do you need anything else, then?"

"Just keep me posted about the contact with the Bureau."

"We'll call you," Jude said. "I'll encrypt the line."

"Thanks. Rayne?" I picked up her suitcase, and it took her a second to look at me. "Let's go."

She shook herself, as if she was trying to wake up from something, before she looked at the others. Her voice was quiet. "Thank you again. And I'm sorry."

"Don't be sorry, Rayne. Be safe," Lucas said.

She followed me out, and I helped her back up into my truck, just like the first time. When I climbed in, she looked over at me, and I didn't think I was supposed to hear her words. "I can't *believe* I'm doing this."

I looked at her and saw the battle brewing in her eyes. "Don't worry, princess. This is going to be fun."

# Chapter 15

**Rayne**

THE SNOW in front of the truck felt like a tunnel we drove through, the veil pierced by Cole's headlights. It was an easy distraction to look at and keep my mind busy, instead of circling the same path of thoughts over and over. Movement, dark, white, the occasional change of the wind's direction.

I didn't know how to feel.

So many things brewed beneath the surface, I felt blank.

Fear. Cold and pure. Never in my life had I experienced this kind of sustained terror. Determination. I wasn't going to roll over and die because this had happened to me. I had a life I enjoyed. It wouldn't be taken away from me because I'd been in the wrong place at the wrong time.

No.

Hesitation. Confusion. I didn't know how to feel about staying with Cole in such close proximity. He wanted to help me. His plea earlier told me that. Nothing about what he said could be a lie. But I wouldn't pretend this was going to be easy.

Cole got under my skin. He pushed my buttons on purpose. He made me want to tear off his clothes and do all the things I expressly told him we *wouldn't* be doing.

*If you ask, Rayne, I'll give you* everything.

I shivered, and it wasn't because the truck was chilly, despite the heater trying its best. Because those words made me want things I couldn't want. Damn him.

This would be like having your favorite cookies on a plate in front of you and being told you weren't allowed to eat them. Because if you *did* eat them, your whole world would come crashing down around you and the cookies would get hurt and you wouldn't be able to have them anymore.

Okay, that was a really bad metaphor, but I was exhausted, and I didn't have the mental energy to make a better one. The point was, Cole and I would be in each other's spaces, and my resolve was already flimsy at best.

The roads we traveled on up into the foothills of the mountains weren't exactly good roads, only made worse by the snow. "You came all the way down here?"

I barely noticed saying it out loud until Cole responded. "Of course I did."

"You…you don't know me, Cole. We've kissed twice. Talked a little." Or a lot, that first night at the bar. "But still, we're practically strangers. Why?"

He was silent for a while before shifting in his seat. "I don't know. I can't explain it, Rayne. You don't *feel* like a stranger to me. I want to know everything about you, even if it doesn't lead anywhere. And all of that aside, I never would have left you alone. The fear in your voice…" He trailed off. "I'll never forget it. It reminds me— I told you I would come if you called. And it's still true. It's not a promise I'll take back."

I didn't know what it reminded him of, and now wasn't the moment to ask him for deep personal information. Still, what he said pulled at my insides. I felt it too. Being with him in close quarters would only make it worse.

*How bad could it be?* the little voice inside whispered. *Just a taste of happiness.*

A different kind of fear gripped me. Older and deeper. The terror of knowing my choices were responsible for so much pain, including my own. I shut my eyes.

Finally, we pulled up to a cabin barely visible in the headlights and the swirling snow. Bigger than I expected and dark. But Cole was right. It certainly was off the grid.

He was out of the truck and opening my door before I could get myself together, and in the cold, his hands felt like raw fire. God, however long we were here was going to be impossible.

Grabbing my suitcase, he guided me inside and flipped on the lights.

I blinked. This wasn't what I had expected when he described it as being in the middle of nowhere and a prepper's paradise. It was…homey. A big, cushy couch and armchair in front of a huge fireplace, complete with a rug in front of it that looked incredibly soft.

The place was split-level, with an elevated area for the bed, and a door that must have led to the bathroom. A galley kitchen and dining table were to my left, and a desk sat in the far corner. All in all, it looked very comfortable. Other than its isolation, it could easily have been a vacation destination. "Wow."

"Welcome to The Phillips Hotel. We just opened, so excuse any remaining mess. But I'm told we have a reputation for excellent hospitality."

His smile told me he was trying to lighten the mood, but I wasn't capable of laughter right now. It was close to five in the morning, and I dragged on my feet.

Cole set the suitcase down and started fastening the impressive display of locks on a front door that was seriously intense, the only visible sign the person who owned this place was on edge.

"The bathroom is there?" I asked.

"Yeah."

I went straight to it and relieved myself before splashing water across my face. This cabin had power, and I didn't hear the telltale whine of a generator in the background. Were there really power lines out this far?

Well, if the owner of the cabin really was a prepper, he probably had underground lines dug—and a couple of generators on top of it. Or maybe there were solar panels on the roof.

I realized I was staring at myself in the mirror. Dazed. Exhausted. I needed to sleep. I couldn't even think about anything anymore.

Once out of the bathroom, I spotted Cole in the kitchen, now without his coat and boots. I stashed mine where he'd put his. He turned, holding a glass of water. "I wasn't sure if you wanted anything more than this or if sleep is higher on the list."

"It is. I feel like my brain is melting inside my skull."

One corner of his mouth tipped up into a smile. "Well, we can't have that."

He handed me the water, and I hadn't realized how thirsty I was. The whole glass was gone in less than ten seconds. "Holy crap."

"Adrenaline will do that to you," he said.

"Yeah. Adrenaline."

I put the glass in the sink, leaning against the counter. Now that my energy was fading, I just...couldn't move. It was easier to stay still than fight the inertia to move.

Cole stepped forward and stopped. "There's only one bed. I'll sleep on the couch. You need the rest."

My head snapped up. "What?"

"I said I'll sleep on the couch," he said, eyebrows rising.

"I'm not sleeping in your bed, Cole."

"It's fine."

I stood straight. "No, it's not. You're already taking me in to keep me from being murdered. I'm not kicking you out of your bed."

He appraised me for a second before shrugging. "Suit yourself."

Something about the way he said it made me think the argument wasn't over, but it was for tonight.

"Okay. I'll see you in the morning."

I found a thick blanket on the back of the couch. I settled on the cushions and pulled it over myself.

"Good night," Cole said. "Who knows? Maybe Daniel will have reached out to the right people at the FBI tomorrow, and everything will be resolved."

"Yeah."

I did hope. I hoped it would be that easy as exhaustion pulled me under.

~

IT WASN'T THAT EASY.

Partially because looking outside the windows of the cabin showed nothing but a wall of whirling white. A full-on blizzard, way too early. I knew it was meant to be a storm, but this?

Our first snow on the ground didn't usually happen for another few weeks. So this was both rare and bad.

Cole didn't have any signal on his phone, so there was no way we could receive any calls right now. I had no doubt that everything was worse because we were higher on the mountain.

The power flickered as I stood by the window. It had been doing that ever since I'd woken up at noon. I hadn't slept in so late in years. Then again, home invasions weren't exactly conducive to good sleep.

"Blizzards are like pots, Rayne. They don't change if they're being watched."

"Because you're so familiar with cold weather and snow?"

Cole sighed, and I deflated a little. I'd been crabby and unfair ever since I woke up. I was out of sorts. I wanted to be with my clients. I wanted to be *home*. I didn't want any of this.

I closed my eyes, pushing down the sudden wave of emotion. Rationally, I knew I shouldn't. I spent time every day telling my clients not to avoid their feelings and to deal with them in both a safe and healthy way. But I didn't know if I was safe. With Cole, sure, but at all?

The power flickered again.

"The guy who owns this place."

"Jimmy?" Cole asked.

I nodded. "Jimmy has a generator, right?"

"He does. A wood-burning one. I think he has a gas one. Or diesel. But I also think he hid it. Because it's nowhere I've seen."

A smile appeared in spite of myself. From what I'd heard of this man so far, hiding the more efficient generator seemed exactly in line with his personality. The wind whipped around the walls, making them groan. Even though the cabin was well-built, the temperature was still dropping, and the power flickering wasn't helping that.

Cole had been sitting in the armchair, reading, but I heard a sound, and when I looked back, he was standing and grabbing his boots. "What are you doing?"

"I should go get the wood for the pile before it gets worse and too cold. I'd hoped it would die down, but the flickers aren't getting better. We'll need it for the generator if the power goes, and we need more for the fire."

"Where is it?"

"About fifty feet down the hill. There's no good place to keep it up against the house. Or maybe Jimmy thinks it's a fire hazard. I'm not sure. But I'll go *Little House on the Prairie* out here and make a path to follow."

He stepped down into the small staircase that led to the basement and opened the door. "I thought you weren't supposed to go down into the holy grail shelter?"

Cole grinned when he came back with a coil of rope over his arm. "What Jimmy doesn't know won't hurt him. And if he's really upset I touched his rope, I'll buy him a new one."

He pulled on his gloves and hat too.

"Do you need help?"

"Not this time, but thank you. If we're here for longer, I'll take you up on it." He winked. "But remember, the Phillips Hotel is unmatched in hospitality. What would the reviews say if we sent our guests out into the snow to get firewood?"

"Cole—"

"I'll be okay, Rayne. It won't take too long, and we'll be buried in firewood."

He slipped out the door and into the howling white. I looked for him out the window, but as soon as he tied off the rope, he was gone.

Utter silence surrounded me, other than the wind, and fear gripped me. It was the first time I'd been alone since last night, and panic clawed up my throat. The room began to close in around me, and I forced breath into my lungs.

I knew what to do to take the edges off a panic attack, but part of me was shocked at the reaction. Last night—

No.

*Stop questioning yourself.*

Forcing myself away from the window to keep looking for Cole, I went back to the couch and wrapped myself in the blanket, thinking about anything else and counting my breaths until he was back and I wasn't alone anymore.

# Chapter 16

**Cole**

FUCK, it was cold.

Good thing I grabbed the rope, because I couldn't see a thing. Already there were probably six inches or more of snow on the ground, and trudging through it, down the small incline to where I knew the wood pile stood, was giving me a workout like I hadn't had in months.

I nearly stumbled over a rock but caught myself at the last second.

*There.*

The vague shadowy outline of the woodpile appeared. And I fell against it, bracing myself in the wind. It was up against a couple of trees, and I triple-knotted the rope around one of the trunks, making sure the line was nearly taut.

As soon as I was done, I filled my arms with wood and went back. But it wasn't enough. Given the intensity of this storm, I didn't know how long it would last, and we couldn't keep coming out here every time we needed a bit of wood.

I pushed the door open just long enough to put the wood inside. Rayne jumped, but I didn't stop. I just waved and shut the door. The space beside it was large and empty, which I'd thought was strange at first but now made sense. It was for things like this.

Keeping my fingers on the rope, I went back.

My coat was good, but it wasn't fully built for this. The snow was soaking through it by the third trip. On the fifth, I was so cold I shook. One more. I could do one more. The amount of wood I brought should last us two days if we were careful, and I hoped we wouldn't need more than that.

The wound in my leg ached with the strain. I hadn't pushed it this far in a long time, and the throbbing nearly put me on my knees. But I was almost there.

Rayne was in the middle of putting more wood on the fire when I pushed in the last time. The wood she had was wet, but it would dry in the flames. Hopefully.

It was so much warmer in here than outside, but still not warm enough. My clothes were soaked and sticking to my skin. I felt like I was made out of ice.

I stared at Rayne. She still wore the pants and T-shirt she'd come here in, and even though I was half frozen, I couldn't stop myself from noticing how fucking beautiful she was.

She looked at me, catching me in the act of staring. "Are you okay?"

"Cold." I shook myself out of the thoughts of her and peeled off my coat, letting it fall to the floor. "I'm about to get naked to warm up faster, so you better turn around if you don't want to see anything."

Rayne stared at me, and a noticeable blush rose to her cheeks before she turned and went to the desk in the corner and sat facing away. "Thank you for doing that."

I stripped off the rest of my clothes, not bothering to do anything with them. I could fix that once I was dry and not shaking. But I grabbed a couple of pieces of wood and set them down in front of the fire to dry more quickly.

"We should be all right for a couple of days." The rug in front of the fireplace was soft, and I mentally thanked Rayne for turning around. I was cold, and it meant I might not make the best impression for the first time she saw me naked.

Smiling, I shook my head, running my fingers through my wet hair. That thought assumed she would see me naked. God, I wanted her to, but I wasn't going to pressure her. At all.

"I hope we won't have to do it again."

"Me too," Rayne said. "But blizzards are unpredictable. Especially ones so out of season. These types can either fizzle —or be way, way worse."

I shuddered, a chill working through me. The heat of the fire felt good, but it would take a while before I was truly warm.

As if the universe looked down at me and wanted to make my life more difficult, the power failed completely. Though it was still midafternoon, the cabin was dark with the storm and the early-fading sunlight.

"Crap," Rayne said.

"It'll be okay." I moved closer to the fire. "Just let me feel a bit less like a popsicle, and we'll get the generator started." Where she was sitting, I saw her wrap her arms around herself. "You should put on some warmer clothes if you have them."

"Right."

She carefully avoided looking in my direction as she grabbed her suitcase and dug through it. The rustle of fabric was such a fucking temptation, I had to focus hard on the embers beneath the flames to pretend both of us weren't naked right now.

A few minutes later, I was dry enough to notice the dropping temperature in the cabin. I grabbed a throw blanket

Rayne hadn't used off the armchair and wrapped myself in it. "Let me get some clothes on, and we'll work on this."

"Okay."

Clothes—dry ones—felt amazing. Like the strange sensation of going swimming for an entire day and then getting your clothes back on. I decided on sweats and a long-sleeved T-shirt since we weren't going anywhere.

I came out of the bathroom to find Rayne laying out my sopping-wet clothes in front of the fire, already having moved the fur rug out of the way. "You don't have to do that."

"They need to dry out," she said. "We don't know what kinds of emergencies we could have, and as much as you annoy me, putting on wet clothes is something I wouldn't wish on anyone. Not even the guys trying to kill me."

I smothered a smile and went to help her, laying out the rest of what was there. "I'll rotate them in a bit. Let me see if I can get the generator worked out." I replaced the wood I had drying so we wouldn't run out.

The generator was in the basement, permanently installed with an exhaust pipe to the outside, cleverly structured so it couldn't be blocked by snow. Jimmy thought of everything.

Thankfully, the wood I'd dried worked. Still damp, but dry enough to catch with kindling. Once the fire was roaring merrily in the small space, the power flicked on ten minutes later. It was still freezing, but there was warm air to aid the fire.

Rayne sat on the couch, wrapped in a blanket, entranced by the flames. "Maybe it wasn't a good idea to come out this far," she said quietly. "This is way worse than we expected."

"It is."

"Based on what you saw, is there any chance of getting down the mountain?"

"Right now?" I looked out the window, and the wall of white appeared even more solid. "No. There's almost a foot of snow. Even if we could see the path down, we'd probably get stuck."

"Yeah." Her voice was quiet. This wasn't the fear I'd seen last night. It was different. She was retreating into herself, and I wasn't sure how to pull her back out.

I perched on the arm of the couch. "Are you hungry?"

"I could eat."

"Want to help me?"

Rayne looked around at the cabin, like she'd been so lost in her own thoughts she wasn't even sure where she was. "Sure. What are we making?"

"Depends on what you feel like eating."

"What do you have?"

I opened the small pantry door and gestured with a bow. "Your wish is my command."

That drew a small smile from her. "I'm guessing we probably don't want anything that will take too much power or energy."

"I'll be honest, I didn't buy anything I thought would take too much of either of those things. I can fend for myself, but cooking isn't something I love to do."

She stood in the doorway of the pantry, so close to me I could smell the shampoo in her hair. Soft and strawberry. This woman was going to have me hard every time I was around a fruit. First cherry, now strawberry. I shifted my body, cursing the fact that I'd put on sweatpants.

I'd promised Rayne I wouldn't pressure her, and I wouldn't. But I was only so strong, and telling my body not to react to her? It would be easier to go out into the blizzard, tell it to stop snowing, and expect it to listen.

"Pasta?" She pulled a box off the shelf and the jar of sauce next to it. "This is easy and sounds good."

"I have some garlic bread in the freezer too."

"The oven?"

I winked. "I think we can eke out enough power to toast it up a little."

We needed to watch the pipes to make sure they didn't freeze. But knowing Jimmy, they were made out of something that would be just fine. If worse came to worst, we could melt some snow and truly go *Little House on the Prairie*, though I'd been joking before.

"What's your favorite food?" I asked.

Rayne looked at me. "What?"

"What's your favorite food?" I asked again, pulling a pot out of the cupboard and filling it with water. The stove was gas, so it didn't draw extra power.

"Why does that matter?"

I laughed. "Just making conversation, Rayne. We're cooking. Thought it might be a good topic for conversation. My favorite meal, for example, is grilled cheese and tomato soup. Simple enough, but I ate it a lot as a kid, and I still love it."

Rayne stared at me for a moment before she finished putting the garlic bread on the cookie sheet she'd found. "Thai," she said. "Pad Thai, usually chicken. I also love Thai iced tea."

"It must be hard to find good Thai food in Montana."

She nodded. "It can be, yes."

I lit the burner and set the water on to boil. "Did you have any while you were in Chicago?"

The name of the city brought a little light to her eyes, which told me enough about where her head was. "No. I didn't have a chance because of the conference."

"Well, if we're ever in Chicago at the same time again, I'll make sure to get you some kick-ass Thai food."

That earned me a smile, which quickly faded.

The water boiled, and I slid the spaghetti into it before turning to Rayne, where she looked out the window. "Favorite color?"

"Purple."

"Favorite kind of music."

She glanced at me. "I don't have one."

"I highly doubt that."

Rayne blinked. "I really don't listen to music often. More podcasts, the news, things like that."

I stepped closer, watching her watch me. She didn't take a step back. "Come on, princess. I can see you driving down the highway, this crazy red hair flying everywhere while you belt something out at the top of your lungs. What is it?"

"I don't." Her entire face flushed.

"Your blush tells me otherwise."

Her gaze hardened, and I was glad. When Rayne was fighting me, she was with me. If she was pissed, at least she was present. "Maybe I'm just done with your bullshit."

"Good thing you're stuck with me, then."

The timer for the garlic bread went off, breaking us apart from where we'd started to drift closer together. She pulled it out and went to put it on the small table while I finished the pasta.

A few more words were exchanged here and there, but Rayne was back to one-word answers and disappearing into her head. I let her fade away, because it was clear she needed it. Not forever, but for now. She hadn't thought about the reality of being stuck out here in hiding, and it was messing with her head.

I didn't blame her.

When we finished eating, I took care of the dishes, made sure the generator was stocked and the fire was banked with wood. By the time all that was done, Rayne was on the couch, back under the blanket, completely asleep.

## Chapter 17

**Cole**

IT WAS FREEZING. The power was still on and the fire was still going, but with the raging storm outside, it wasn't enough.

Even under the multiple blankets on the bed, I couldn't get fully warm. The wind cut through every crevice it could find, stealing heat, life, and happiness itself.

Before I slept, I'd made sure Rayne was covered in more blankets. She was buried in at least three of them and was next to the fire, but I still heard her stirring. She wasn't comfortable, and neither was I.

I looked at the clock on the bedside table. It wasn't even midnight.

Turning on my back, I stared at the ceiling. This was ridiculous. Neither of us was going to get any kind of good sleep, and this was no longer a situation where principle ruled over practicality.

I stripped back the blankets and went to the living room,

striding around the couch and lifting Rayne. Multiple blankets and all. She stirred, clearly awake. "What are you doing?"

"I'm bringing you to bed."

"Cole—"

"I can hear your teeth chattering all the way from the other room." I set her down on the side of the bed opposite mine. "I'm cold too. We both need the warmth, and we'll both sleep better. Basic survival, combining resources."

I slipped back under the covers, spreading her blankets over the ones on the bed so they all covered us both. Already, it was better. Reaching across under the blankets, I tugged Rayne toward me, folding her body into mine until her face was tucked beneath my chin.

She blew out a shaky breath. "I'm still not having sex with you."

Laughing, I held her tighter, enjoying the relief of warmth. "Don't worry, princess. I didn't expect it. But don't lie and say this isn't better already."

She didn't.

We were both freezing, but slowly, the pocket beneath the blankets where we were warmed up, far better than it could when we were alone. Our bodies relaxed, and it no longer felt like an awkward embrace for survival. Now I was aware of how soft Rayne's body was against mine and resisted the urge to stroke my hand down her spine.

This was so much better.

I drifted, dozing, but I couldn't sleep. Not when I finally exactly where I needed to be. Based on the way Rayne kept moving subtly as well, she wasn't sleeping either.

"You still awake, princess?"

"Why do you call me that?"

Nerves stuttered in my chest. It had just started naturally, and I hadn't fully examined why. But I wasn't sure I was ready to admit the depth of it. Princess because she ruled over me already, no matter how little had happened between us. Princess because I wanted to treat her like one. Princess because she glided through life, easily distant, and I wanted to be the one who broke the barriers she kept up. "Why not?"

"I'm not a princess," she murmured. "Not even close."

"Why do you say that?"

She stayed quiet, and I gently shifted her closer, leaning back a little so she rested on my chest. She didn't resist.

The real question I'd been dying to ask hovered on my lips. Was this the right time?

*Yes.*

Here in the dark and the warmth, it was easier to admit things that were difficult. Because this didn't seem real. We were in a pocket world that would disappear when the sun rose and the snow quieted.

"Can I ask you something?" I whispered, my lips brushing her temple. It could have been a coincidence, but I felt her shiver.

"Yes."

"Why do you keep pushing me away?" I kept the words gentle. "Why do you keep saying you can't? I know I'm an arrogant prick and I get under your skin. But while I'm working on the arrogant thing, I won't apologize for riling you up. I love the blush on your cheeks when you're about to strangle me."

We both laughed softly.

"There's something standing in between us, and it's not me. I can't explain to you how I know, but I do. Please tell me why, so I can understand."

Rayne tightened her hands on my back, clinging to me even if she wasn't fully aware of it. "You noticed?"

"Rayne." Her entire tone was deflection. Whatever went through her head when she talked about this, it scared her. "For tonight, let's pretend we're not who we are. There's no one outside of this room but the two of us. Let's not lie, and let's not keep up the shields we normally have. Please."

It was as honest as I could be with her. My vulnerability lay on my chest like an open book.

She was silent and still for a long time. So long, I wondered if she'd actually fallen asleep. Then, so softly I barely heard it above the wind, she spoke. "You scare me."

My body went rigid, and her hand moved to my chest. "No, not like that. Never like that… You scare me because of what you bring out in me."

I relaxed again, the terror in my limbs seeping out of me. If I'd made her afraid of me in that way—like I would ever hurt her—I would never forgive myself. I could be an asshole, no question, but I would never hurt her or push her beyond what she really wanted. Even in the cold, if she refused to be in this bed, I would let her go.

"Why?" I asked her.

She groaned, hiding her face in my chest like it wasn't me she was hiding from. "Because you make me *feel*. You make me *want*. And especially now, I can't do it, Cole. I can't let you in, because if I do, I'll lose you."

"You'll never lose me, Rayne."

"Don't say that," she breathed. "You can't. Because bad things happen to people I love. I know it's a strange thing to hear from a therapist, but I would rather be without you than fall in love with you and lose you forever."

It took all my focus to keep my body relaxed and easy. The pain in her voice was palpable. She'd gone through something, and I wanted to protect her from it, even though it was clearly in the past.

"Who did you lose?"

Rayne shook her head, hair tickling my chin. "Not now," she whispered. "I'm not ready for it, and even with us all alone, you haven't earned that."

I understood. We weren't at the place to share our darkest secrets. Or at least, she wasn't. But I could give her an offering to show her I was serious and to tell her I got what she meant.

"I haven't told you why I joined the FBI, have I?"

"No."

Clearing my throat, I moved, drawing my hand down her side and moving her even farther onto me.

"Well, I definitely understand what it's like to do things because of people you love. My brother, Jamie—" I swallowed. "My brother was killed by someone a lot like Simon Derine. He hadn't even done anything. They thought he was someone else. But he called me, terrified. I was still in the military, but I was home, and I couldn't get to him in time."

"I'm sorry."

"It was a long time ago."

Slowly, Rayne drew her hand up my chest and slid it back around my side where it had been. "It doesn't mean it hurts less."

"Yeah." I took a long, slow breath to ease the ache in my chest. "You're right. I was close to leaving the service, and when I was approached to join the Bureau, I did it because I wanted to stop people like the Riders. I didn't want anyone else's brother to die because of assholes like him who thought guns and drugs were more important than people's lives."

My voice choked in my chest, and I fought the rising emotion, even though we'd agreed to be honest. No matter how long ago it had happened, when I focused on it, everything was still raw.

"But I couldn't even tell my own partner was dirty. Right in front of me the whole time, and I never questioned or suspected. Even when I *had* a suspicion, it was justified. I let myself be mollified and talked off the ledge. I failed so utterly and completely. The entire reason I joined the Bureau feels like a joke."

Then, the piece of it I'd never fully shared with anyone, not even myself, spilled out. "Part of me wants them to expel me. It would be a fitting punishment for…being so foolish. For failing."

Rayne was so still, I felt like she might break. "You didn't fail."

More people than she had told me that since the take-down. It didn't make it real. Because no matter how many people told me I wasn't a failure, I was. "It doesn't feel that way."

"You took a bullet in the leg, Cole. As soon as you knew the truth, you did everything you could to save the person who needed it most. You brought Emma and Daniel home alive. That's not a failure. That's being a hero."

Discomfort squirmed inside. "I'm not a hero, Rayne."

"And I'm not a princess, but if you're going to call me one, then I can call you the other."

I chuckled. She had a point there, and I wouldn't fight her on it. "Fine. But more to the point, if you don't think I failed, then neither did you. I know what happened to my brother wasn't my fault, even if I hold myself responsible for it.

"Whatever happened to your people wasn't your fault either. Because loving someone is never a bad thing."

She was quiet for a long time. And when I heard her voice again, breath brushing against my throat, it was low and sleepy. "What's your favorite color?"

I smiled in the dark. She hadn't returned any of my ques-tions earlier, and she didn't need to. But this felt like more. It felt like an olive branch and a reaching-out and both of us clinging to something nameless, breathless, and desperate.

"Green."

"Favorite music?"

"Classic rock," I admitted. "I'm an open book, Rayne. Whatever you want to know about me? I'll tell you."

"Anything?" Her voice was a tiny murmur.

I risked everything, pulling her as close as I could against my chest without crushing her. "I played water polo in high school before I went into the Navy. I would rather do literally any other exercise besides running. When I was a kid, I owned an iguana named Fred, and I cried when he died." Rayne's body went soft and pliant in my arms, her breathing evening out and slowing.

"I've always wanted to travel to Africa, and winter is my favorite season. But maybe the most important thing. As soon as I saw you, I felt like I knew you. You scare me too, princess, because I'm so far gone, this hero would do anything for you."

Rayne moved in her sleep, shifting to be more comfortable against me. Even if it was never more than this, Rayne felt safe with me, and after everything, that was all I could ever ask.

# Chapter 18

**Rayne**

*SMOKE.*

Why did it smell like smoke?

I came to consciousness full of warmth and completely relaxed on a very comfortable pillow. When I opened my eyes, it was dark. Then I realized that was simply because my head was tucked under the comforter.

The pillow under me moved.

*Oh my god.*

I was on Cole's chest, clinging to him like he was the world's biggest body pillow. He held me too, hands gripping me tighter than I thought one could while sleeping. Our legs tangled together.

Last night felt like a fever dream. Did any of that conversation really happen? Or was it just my cold-fueled imagination?

Clearly, some of it happened, or I would still be on the couch and not in this nest of delicious warmth with a man I should not be this close to.

Lifting my head from beneath the edge of the blanket, I suddenly remembered what woke me. The air in the cabin was hazy with smoke, and I could smell it. Across the room, the fire in the fireplace was down to coals, the air freezing, but that wasn't where the smoke came from. It came from...

The basement.

"Cole," I croaked, untangling myself from him and desperately wishing I hadn't because away from him, the air was frigid. "Cole, something's wrong."

He opened his eyes and came alert in the way only the military guys I knew could. "Shit."

Leaping out of the bed, he was down in the basement in a second. Coughing sounded, and he came back, his shirt over his mouth and nose. "We need to clear the air. Can you get the big fire going again?"

"Yeah."

I sprang into action, ignoring the cold quickly seeping into my fingers and toes. The only reason we had been cuddled together like that this morning was because we needed to stay warm. There was no other reason. None.

Not because we'd both made ourselves vulnerable and dropped the masks we showed everyone else. Not because he'd allowed me to see through the charade and admit the truth.

No.

The wood was much drier now, thankfully, and it didn't take long to get the flames rising again. Cole opened two windows a sliver on either side of the cabin, and the smoke began to slide out, clearing the air. I pulled a blanket around my shoulders and huddled near the fire, waiting.

Cole grabbed wood and disappeared with his makeshift mask again. But it wasn't long before he was back, face grim, shutting the windows now that the air was clear.

He grabbed a blanket from the bed and came to sit, turning me toward him so we were knee to knee. "You look like you're about to tell me someone died, and considering there's no power…"

"I don't know what's going on with it, but it won't turn back on. Even with a fire going inside it, there's no power coming from it. I wish I knew how to fix it, but I don't." He smiled briefly. "Hurts my manly feelings a little, but I'm not an engineering guy. I'm sorry, Rayne."

"We have a fire."

"I grabbed this." He held out a phone that looked like a brick. A satellite phone. "Saw it was down there before. But it doesn't have a signal either."

Yesterday, I'd been nervous. Now, I was afraid. We were safe enough, but it was cold, and the wood pile was smaller than I had thought. It wasn't burning faster, but we needed it more, so it would go quickly now that it was our only source of heat.

"Hey," Cole said. He reached for me, his hand slipping behind my neck. His fingers were cool but not freezing since we were wrapped in blankets. "We're going to be fine. We still have water, and I bought plenty of things that don't need to be cooked."

"Yeah." I couldn't speak through the fear in my chest. This was unfamiliar ground for me. I didn't have many fears, and the last few days had been nothing but. I didn't like it.

Cole brought the rest of the blankets over to the couch, and we moved it closer to the fireplace itself. He grabbed granola bars too, and I couldn't even look at him. It felt like the same vulnerability as before, but in the hazy light of day, it was so much harder.

We didn't speak, but we settled together under the blankets, sharing warmth, and just breathing. Cole got his book and read, occasionally checking the satellite phone for a signal, and I stared into the flames and dozed.

Just like I thought, the woodpile dwindled quickly in our

attempts to keep the fire roaring. By the time it was midafternoon, my stomach swam with nerves. The pile of wood
wouldn't get us through tonight at this rate, and the wind
didn't show signs of slowing.

I eased off the couch and went to my suitcase, pulling out
the thickest clothes I'd brought with me.

"What are you up to?"

"We need more wood," I said. "It's not going to last."

Cole stood from the couch instantly. "You don't have to go.
I'll go."

"Your clothes are barely dry from last time," I said. "You
put the rope up, right? Straight line?"

"Yes. But, Rayne—"

I shoved my foot into one boot. "We're both in this
together, and I want to help. It's my turn."

"I don't want you to get that cold."

"I'm not a damsel in distress, Cole. I don't need saving. I'm
a grown-ass adult. And if we're doing this together, then we're
doing it together. You said you'd take me up on the offer."

One look at his face told me he wasn't happy about it, but
he didn't say anything as I bundled myself up to the gills. Cole
was only humoring me because we were stuck here together,
but I took the win.

"Be careful, please," he said as I reached for the door. Did
I imagine his voice was raw?

"I will."

The second I stepped outside and shut the door behind
me, I wondered if I'd made a mistake. Even with all the insula-
tion, the wind cut through my coat, chilling me to the bone.
The rope extended into the blustery white, and I followed it. I
had to shuffle through the growing piles of snow. My core and
legs *burned* with the effort.

The path Cole made yesterday was pretty much gone, but
I would take anything that made it easier.

I stumbled into the wood pile when I found it. At least it was here, and I'd made it. Good. I picked up as much as I could manage and trudged my way back, Cole immediately taking the wood from me when I made it to the door. How many trips had he made yesterday? It was probably six or seven. Holy shit, I didn't know if I'd make as many. I already felt as if I'd run five miles just going there and back.

But as long as I kept moving, I would be okay. It was stopping that was the problem.

*Fight the inertia, Rayne.*

With my hand on the rope, I went back. One step at a time. My toe hit something hard, and my momentum along with my bulky clothes pitched me forward. *Shit!*

I pushed myself up, blinking against the wind, and my stomach sank. The rope was gone. Or rather, I saw it being carried away by the wind. I must have broken it in the fall.

That wasn't good.

My saving grace was the path I'd already made with my body. I couldn't fully see it, but I could roughly feel the edges where my knees connected with the walls of snow.

When I got back to the cabin, I'd grab the rope again and fix it. Or have Cole get me more from the basement to redraw the line in case it had snapped and not just unraveled.

Inch by inch, I made my way down the path, but I should have been there by now. I thought I was still in the trail of snow I'd made, but it was hard to tell and even harder with my sudden, growing panic. It clawed at my throat, making it even harder to breathe.

A few more feet. I'd go a few more feet before going back the way I came. It had to be close.

Snow shifted beneath my feet, and I fell suddenly, sliding down a hill. My foot caught on something, pain shrieking through it as it yanked me to a stop. Oh god, it hurt. Moving it at all sent skittering lightning bolts of pain through my leg.

It didn't feel broken. Small favors. But twisted? Yes. For sure.

Slowly, I moved it enough to get it free of whatever held it, groaning the whole time. Upright. I was upright. That was good. I pushed myself up and fell down again, pain blazing brighter than all the surrounding white. *Fuck*, this was bad.

But my ankle wasn't the thing that had me shivering more than from the cold. I was in the middle of a blizzard, injured, and disoriented. And I had no idea where to go.

# Chapter 19

**Cole**

I WATCHED out the window for any sign of movement to tell me Rayne was on her way back, but I saw nothing. This was too long. Much longer than her first trip to the wood and back.

She should have returned long before now, and my instincts told me something was *wrong*. The pile of wood was about fifty feet from the front door of the cabin. Nothing in good weather, a rough distance in bad. But it wasn't impossible, especially with the guiding line we had. No, something was wrong.

Where was she?

I didn't want to overstep her boundaries. Rayne was clear. She wasn't a damsel in distress, and I didn't want to treat her like one. But if something happened and I didn't make it to her in time? I didn't know if I could live with myself either. Rayne wasn't Jamie, but at times like this, I couldn't fight the memories.

Five more minutes.

A dark streak flew through the air. What the hell was that?

In the shifting snow, I focused and found the object again, whipping through the air.

My entire body went cold.

It was the rope.

Blowing in the fucking wind.

There wasn't nearly enough length on that piece to make it to the wood. It had broken, snapped, or even worse, someone cut it.

Sprinting into the basement, I grabbed more rope. Never in my life had I gotten dressed that fast. Every cell in my body screamed at me to move. Faster. She was in trouble, and she needed help.

*Please*, I begged the universe. *Please let her be alive.*

It hadn't been long enough for her to freeze, but this was a mountain in a whiteout blizzard. Anything could happen.

I tied the new rope off where the other one hung limp and tied the other end around myself three times. With both of us out here, I couldn't risk losing the second rope.

"Come on, Rayne," I muttered, pushing in the direction I knew she'd gone. "Where are you?"

There was no sign of her on the path she'd left straight to the woodpile. The other half of the rope whipped in the wind, snapped in half. Where had it broken?

"*Rayne!*"

Every ounce of my strength went into calling her name. Grabbing the broken rope, I walked it back toward the cabin until it was nearly taut. Maybe I could find her if I found where the split was.

"*Rayne, where are you?*"

I called her name until my throat was raw, terror rising under my skin. What if I didn't find her? What if I was too late and she froze to death alone out here?

One more time, I screamed her name, and more than the wind answered me. "*Cole.*"

Thank fuck. Where was she?

I turned toward where I thought the voice had come from. "Rayne."

"*I'm here!*"

There. A darker spot against the blinding white. Barely visible and clearly down a drop... My heart stuttered. She'd fallen. Whatever had caused her to move off the path and fall, I would destroy it.

It took way too long to get to her, inch by agonizing inch, making sure I didn't fall too and doom us both. I slid the last foot down beside her. "Rayne."

"I fell," she said. "I'm so sorry. I fell. My ankle. I tried, and I can't put weight on it."

I shook my head. "It doesn't matter," I said. "We're going to be okay. I've got you."

Rayne stared at me like she wasn't fully with me.

"Do you believe me?"

"Yes." She nodded.

Pushing myself to my feet, I moved, shifting so I faced the hill once more. Adrenaline spun through me like a hurricane, a tornado stronger than the storm we were in. I could probably do that "lift a car off a baby" thing right about now.

Rayne whimpered as I pulled her up off the ground and into my arms, and rage shattered across my vision. She was hurt. Nothing could make it better unless I got her back to the cabin. And I would. We were going to get through this.

"We're going to go slow," I told her, still having to yell over the wind. "We'll get back. Grab the rope around my waist. You'll keep us on course."

She used the hand not around my neck to grab the rope, gathering the slack across her chest. And we went. Step by agonizing step. All the way back to the cabin. The shadowy shape through the snow was a welcome sight.

"Here we are," I said, shouldering the door open, nearly stumbling with the force of it.

Moving quickly, I set her down in front of the fire before ditching the rope around my waist and kneeling in front of her. "Can I touch you? I need to touch you, Rayne. You're freezing."

Her skin was so pale it was nearly blue, her teeth chattering. "Y-yes."

Boots first. This would be hard because of her ankle, but I needed to get the rest of her clothes off and see the damage we were dealing with. One boot got tossed behind me, and then it was time for the other one. "I'm going to be as gentle as I can, princess. It's going to hurt. I'm so sorry, but we have to get it off."

Rayne moaned in pain. "Do it."

The sounds coming out of her made me want to kill something. They brought out the warrior inside me and the urge to *protect*. But Rayne needed a different kind of protector right now.

I peeled the sock away and cleared my facial expression. Her ankle was swollen all to hell, red and angry in comparison to her cold, soaked skin. "Okay, princess. That was the hardest part. Now we have to get you warm."

Her coat was sopping. If possible, more soaked through than my clothes had been yesterday. Piece by piece, I took her clothes off. The number of times I'd imagined this, and it wasn't the least bit sexy. Her body was shaking she was so cold.

Snatching a blanket off the couch, I wrapped her in it once her clothes were off, shifting her closer to the fire, where I added another log.

First aid. I knelt, snowmelt pooling around my knees as I

held her foot. "I need to see if it's broken," I said quietly. "I'm going to be so careful."

The smallest movement made her shudder and whimper in pain. But the way it *did* move, I didn't think it was broken. Luckily. We'd tended to more than one injury by ourselves in the Navy. Wrapping it was easy, but it wouldn't do much. At the very least, it would make her more comfortable.

"Here," I said, placing a pillow under her foot. "Keep this elevated."

"Where are you going?" Rayne's voice was strangled with panic.

I picked the rope up off the floor and wrapped it around my waist again. "We still need wood. I'll be right back. Promise." If I didn't get out of the cabin right this second, I wouldn't be able to force myself back into the freezing void. So, I went. I reattached the rope to the tree by the dwindling wood pile, and I brought back as much wood as I could. Until my limbs shook and I thought I might be seeing things in the snow.

My clothes joined Rayne's on the floor, and I grabbed my own blanket, settling beside her on the rug and putting more wood on the fire. "We're good," I said. "We're going to be fine."

Rayne didn't say anything. She stared into the flames much like she'd done for most of the day before she'd gone outside. Her foot rested on the pillow, and her shoulders rose and fell with each breath. But besides that? Still as a statue.

"What happened out there?" I asked. "How did you fall? Is it something we can fix?"

She didn't say anything at all.

"Rayne, are you okay? Please talk to me."

In the glow of the fire, her cheeks turned pink, but she didn't look at me. Realization suddenly dawned. She was embarrassed. Before she'd gone out to bring in the wood, she'd made a stand about helping and being an equal partner, and it had gone to hell.

"Rayne," I said, softly this time. When she still didn't react, I moved the pillow with her foot toward me as gently as I could, turning her body to face me. Even now, she wouldn't meet my gaze.

"It's all right, Rayne. I promise."

"No, it's not."

"Listen to me." I tucked a finger under her chin and lifted her eyes to mine. Misery, pain, and embarrassment filled them. "This could have happened to either of us. There's no guarantee I wouldn't have fallen in that exact spot. And while you being in pain makes me want to tear the world limb from limb, if it had been me, it would have been so much harder for you to find me and help me get back here."

"And then you went and got the wood too," she whispered. "You must be freezing. If I'd just let you do it like you wanted to—"

I moved, slipping my hand behind her neck. "No. We, of all people, know there's no use in dwelling on the way things could have been. There's only the way things are, and right now, we're alive. We're both safe, if a little worse for wear." Shaking my head, I held myself back from gathering her in my arms, because it was the only thing that felt right.

"You don't have anything to be embarrassed about," I told her.

Rayne looked at me, her expression one I'd never seen before. It was hope, filled with determination. Bracing herself so her ankle was okay, Rayne closed the distance between us and kissed me.

# Chapter 20

**Rayne**

I KISSED HIM.

I kissed him, and there was nothing in the world I wanted more than to *keep* kissing him. This thing between us Cole kept talking about? I was done ignoring it.

Cold still clung to my limbs and my ankle ached, but this was more important. I needed this.

"Rayne, wait," Cole whispered.

"No."

He took my face in his hands. "Wait, princess," he breathed the words before kissing me again, like the magnets between us couldn't be pulled apart. "Are you sure about this? I can and will wait for you. I don't want you to rush into this because of what happened."

I pulled him closer. "It is that," I said. "But it's not *just* that. I'm tired of fighting it."

He grinned. "So you finally admit there's something here."

"Don't ruin it."

"I wouldn't dream of it."

A different kind of chill rippled through me. "As long as you know going in what happens to the people around me."

"I'm not afraid of something that's not going to happen."

"It will."

He kissed me lightly. "Now who's ruining it?"

Nothing but the sound of the wind surrounded us as we came together. Cole's kiss was already familiar, but now it was also different and filled with determination. Power that hadn't been present before. How much had he held back the last time we'd kissed?

I pulled his shoulders, leaning back, and he stopped me. "Not yet."

"What?"

"I've waited a long time to have you. We have all the time in the world right now, and I intend to memorize you slowly. Not taking a single moment for granted. Especially when you look so fucking beautiful in this firelight."

My face and chest flushed with heat, banishing the last vestiges of frost from my bones. "Cole."

His lips met my temple. "Close your eyes, princess. Let me take care of you."

Eyes fluttering closed, I let out a shuddering breath. Cole brushed his hands down over my shoulders, mouth following the same path slowly. He kissed over my cheekbones, brushing the side of my lips and my jaw to my neck. He sucked on my pulse point, and shivers that had nothing to do with snow followed.

My body was still hidden beneath the blanket, and he couldn't see the way my nipples hardened under his touch or how I was suddenly aware of every texture. The pads of his fingers and the softness of the rug we sat on.

Cole followed my collarbone with his lips, teasing my shoulder before slipping his fingers under the edge of the blanket and peeling it away. "You weren't kidding about the slow thing."

"I never joke when it comes to you."

He leaned me back on the rug, supporting me so my ankle didn't jar and cause me pain as he came with me. His own blanket slipped away, and I wasn't shy about looking. The temptation yesterday when he sat here just like this had driven me crazy, wondering what he'd looked like when I'd imagined it so many times.

Now? I couldn't see all of him, but what I did see was lean and strong and didn't hold a candle to my imagination. Not even the glimpse of him in the Resting Warrior gym had been a good comparison to Cole up close.

"Careful looking at me like that, Rayne."

I raised an eyebrow. "How am I looking at you?"

"Your eyes are hotter than the fire."

"What happens if I'm not careful?"

Leaning down, he licked the hollow of my throat. "Keep looking at me like that, and I won't be able to go slow."

Pleasure spiraled down through me, warming my gut and waking up yearnings I'd desperately tried to ignore. "I never said I wanted to go slow."

"Good thing I have excellent self-control."

"Control is overrated."

"Mmm." He hummed into my skin, kissing down between my breasts. "When you're not in pain, I'll happily lose control with you, princess. I will take you against the wall. Bent over the table. I want to put you in every position imaginable and fuck you so hard you'll feel me for days. We both need that, and it'll happen.

"But right now, I need to be soft and slow, and savor the fact that you're alive. I thought I'd lost you." His voice scraped along my skin. "Out in the snow when I couldn't find you, I was out of my mind, thinking you would freeze alone and it would have been my fault."

Any sound I could make stalled in my throat. Cole's mouth closed over my nipple, tongue sliding over my skin. The fire under my skin went against Cole's slow and deliberate movements. I wanted him to *move* and *take* and *fuck*.

"Cole—"

He sucked slowly, every pull of his mouth adding to the arousal burning under my skin.

"You're going to drive me crazy."

"Now you're getting the idea."

"Please?"

Sucking hard, he released one nipple and teased the other. "Not this time. Beg me all you want, princess. This time, we're going slow."

His words echoed in my head.

*I'm the man who's going to challenge you and make you blush and tease you, because I don't think you have anyone in your life who does that.*

He was right. People didn't think they could challenge someone like me. Or play with me because I was a therapist. I was serious. Full of gravity. They yielded when they were allowed to push.

Cole didn't yield. The man had no fear of pushing on the walls I'd unconsciously built. I was the person who helped everyone else dismantle their walls, but I had no one to do it for me. He would, and he would be there to catch me when I inevitably fell.

I tried not to be terrified.

Dragging his lips down my skin, he lowered himself onto my body, giving me his weight and pulling his hands down my ribs. He deposited gentle kisses as he went, and then he let out a groan. "You're just as soft as I imagined."

"You imagined me?" My voice was breathless in the quiet crackle of the fire and the howl of the surrounding storm.

"I tried not to," he admitted. "But yes, I did." Cole's lips brushed over my hipbone, his fingers digging into my ass. "And I'm about to find out if what I imagined you tasting like is real."

"Cole, you don't have to do that. It might take a while."

I hadn't been with anyone other than my vibrator in a long time, but even when I had been, I wasn't someone who came easily. Too much went on in my head for me to let go.

"You're right." He pulled my legs apart with infinite gentleness, making sure to lift my ankle first. "I don't *have* to do anything. Putting my mouth on you? I want to do that. My mouth is watering, Rayne. I want to feel you come all over my tongue, and I don't care how long it takes. Even if you don't come, I want my face soaked with you."

I swore and felt his smile pressing into my inner thigh before he put his mouth on me. Tiny, delicate strokes of his tongue, teasing my clit and lower, tracing my entrance. My breath shuddered. "Cole."

As if my name unlocked him, he sucked on my clit, groaning like he'd been starving and I was his favorite meal. "Rayne." He whispered my name into my skin. "*Fuck me*, I want to drown in you."

"I—" I swallowed against the thick lump in my throat. I'd been cold out there, but my body had drenched me in sweat to try to compensate. I hadn't showered in days now. No matter what he said, this couldn't be fun for him.

My legs tried to close, and he tapped my inner thigh. "Don't even think about it."

I closed my eyes.

He moved, and the light shifted. "Look at me."

Cole was back over me, face-to-face. "I lost you. Where'd you go?"

I just shook my head. It was a beautiful moment. We'd joked about ruining it, but here I was, actually ruining it.

Nerves exploded in my stomach, and my gaze flickered away to the ceiling. The fire. Anything else but him.

"Rayne." He pressed his forehead to mine. "I need you to hear me. Are you listening?"

"Yeah."

His cheek brushed mine. "I don't know what's going on in that beautiful mind of yours or what it's telling you. Whether it's about you or me or what I want, it's not my voice. Understand?"

I nodded, emotion scraping my insides.

"I see you," he whispered. "I see all of you. The cracks in the mask you try to hide because I have those same cracks."

"Cole."

He kissed me, stealing my breath and the words out of my mouth. "Do you trust me?"

How could I not trust him? Cole Phillips took a bullet to save my friends. He hid me when I had no other place to go. He risked his own life to save mine. "Yes."

"Good. You take care of everyone else. Let me take care of you."

That made a smile spread over my face in spite of my nerves. "Sex is taking care of me?"

"Absolutely, it is. Now, if you'll excuse me, I wasn't finished with my meal."

He was between my legs again in a second, using his tongue on me in ways I'd never felt before. Heat bloomed in my gut. Cole knew what he was doing. "Do I even want to know how you know how to do this so well?"

Cole chuckled, the vibrations of his laugh making me gasp. "I don't know what you mean. But I'll tell you I practiced on a pillow."

"Bullshit." An impossible laugh burst out of me, and then I wasn't laughing, because Cole's tongue curled under my clit and made me see sparks in the air that weren't from our fire.

There was no more talking after that. My eyes closed, heat burst outward, and I sank into myself. Cole proved he wasn't joking when he said he didn't care about time or progress. He consumed me with a fervor I didn't understand and still didn't fully believe.

One shoulder pushed under my good leg, giving deeper access. Even more when he shoved his hands under my ass and held me like the feast he thought I was.

Gentle and then not. Fierce and then retreating. I wasn't sure how I could describe a tongue as loving, but that's what it felt like.

I opened my eyes and found Cole's eyes on mine. More heat in them than the fire beside us. He slid his hands out from under me, locking our fingers together, anchoring me. Pulling me toward him. Giving me the strength and support I needed to let go completely.

Cole closed his eyes and groaned, sucking so deep I saw stars and fell into bliss. I arched my hips into him, and he didn't let me go, teasing me through the orgasm that felt absolutely impossible—and even after, when my body sagged to the blankets.

"I don't want to stop," he murmured against my thigh. "I'll stay right here, tasting your pleasure, princess."

A strangled sound came out of my throat. "You can't."

"Yes, I can." He kissed the skin of my stomach. "Until you believe it."

His mouth made a path back up my body until he reached my neck. Our hands still tangled together, he stretched them over my head and settled between my thighs. "More importantly, I didn't plan for this. I don't have any condoms, and if you don't want to take the risk, we won't. I haven't been with anyone since before I met you, and the last time I was tested, my results were clear. But I will happily, *happily* worship at the altar that is your pussy for the rest of our time in this cabin."

Kisses on my cheek. My temple. My jaw. Every touch overwhelmed and astounded me. If anything, this showed me the whole truth.

The man I'd first met was gone.

This was who Cole Phillips was when given space to breathe and find himself. Come to terms with what he'd been through and feel what he'd done to others.

"No," I whispered. "I want you."

"Are you sure?"

"I haven't—" My breath hitched. "It's been a long time."

Cole kissed me slowly. "Would you hate me if I told you I enjoyed hearing that?"

"Going alpha male on me?" I managed a smile, though my breath was short.

"Maybe a little. But as much as I like the idea of no one having touched your body in a while, I like it more that you're willing to share it with me."

In his words, I heard the hesitancy and the shame. The feeling of being undeserving. I blinked back tears and wrapped my arms around his neck. "Stay with me. Please."

Moving slowly, Cole fit himself against me and slid home.

## Chapter 21

**Cole**

*OH MY FUCKING GOD.*

My head dropped into the hollow of Rayne's neck, allowing me to breathe in her scent. Strawberries and sex. Feel the heat and the sweat on her skin that I put there.

But being inside her?

I was blind.

My whole body shuddered, not used to the feeling of *coming home*. It wasn't my imagination. This was different. So much *more* than I'd ever thought about, and I was truly, entirely fucked.

There was no way back from this.

*Mine.*

The deepest part of me declared this woman as a part of me, and though I knew I had no claim to her, losing her now would ruin me.

And I would take the ruin for a little piece of this heaven. But god, I hoped we could last.

"Rayne." I whispered her name against her lips. "You feel…"

Her neck strained upward, and I licked her skin, needing to taste more of her. All of her. One orgasm between her thighs wasn't nearly enough to satisfy the craving.

I rocked into her, and the sound of her trembling breath was everything. This woman was the bravest person I'd ever met in my fucking life. It took everything not to drive into her like my deepest desires told me to, but I wouldn't hurt her.

Lifting her thigh, I wrapped my fingers around it before curling her injured leg around my hips. "Does that hurt?"

"I don't think anything can hurt right now."

My tone was a warning. "Rayne."

"No, it doesn't hurt."

"Good."

When I moved, she moved, and then we moved together. Slow, aching, and perfectly in sync. I watched her face, savoring the little expressions of pleasure. It was all I wanted—her pleasure.

Little changes in angles until she lost her breath. "Right there, princess?"

Rayne bit her lip, nodding.

I bent down and brushed my lips over her ear. "Do you like to be loud? Do you like hearing me talk to you?"

"I'm not good at this."

Capturing her mouth with mine, I kissed her until her muscles eased once again, rolling my hips exactly against the spot that made her moan. "There's nothing to be bad at. I love hearing you. I love feeling you."

"I—"

Kissing her again, I swallowed her words. In this moment, I wouldn't let her doubt herself or think there was anything she could do wrong. Her hair shone bright in the firelight, the glow of her skin and the twinkle in her eyes capturing all of my attention. She was so fucking beautiful, she stole my breath.

I pulled her leg farther around me so I could push deeper. Harder. Drive her into breathless pleasure.

We fell into the rhythm, growing faster together.

Rayne stifled a moan, and I pressed her hands harder into the floor. "Don't hide from me, Rayne. Let me hear you. I fucking love those sounds."

Her next moan was louder, and it drove all my remaining blood to my cock. "God, you feel good," I breathed the words into her neck, thrusting harder, grinding down to drive her higher.

I let her hands go, scooping my arms under her shoulders, cradling her head. She dropped her hands to my shoulders, nails digging in. Those little breaths I recognized from her first orgasm started again, the heat of her mouth grazing my neck.

*Yes.* I didn't dare say anything or stop. I needed her to come more than anything in this life. No stopping, no speeding up or slowing down.

Rayne fell apart, body clenching down on me as she gasped and moaned, pulling me down to her and finally showing me everything.

It was the most beautiful thing I'd ever seen.

Lightning barreled down my spine, pleasure slamming into me like a train. My mouth crushed hers to stop myself from completely unleashing every bit of lust I'd had for her since the first moment I saw her. It went on for longer than I'd ever had before.

We came back to ourselves gradually, kisses slowing, bodies still connected. Words tumbled around in my head, but none of them felt right. None of them felt *real*.

"I don't know what to say, except sex has never made me speechless before," I whispered against her lips.

Rayne wrapped her arms around my neck. "Don't go anywhere," she said. "Please."

"I'm not." She had no idea how true that was. I wasn't going to leave her unless she ordered me to go.

"Right now, I mean." She drifted her hands over my shoulders and down my ribs, cheeks flushing. "I—"

"What?"

Her breath shook. Part of me hated seeing her so nervous, and the other part of me reveled in the fact that she trusted me. "I like this part," she said. "I mean, I like all of it. But I like feeling…" Rayne closed her eyes. "Your weight. The heaviness. Feeling solid, like you're not going anywhere. It never lasts long enough." The last few words were mumbled, and she glanced toward the fire.

The idea that someone would roll over and go to sleep after being with a woman like Rayne made me see red. She would get sick of how much I wanted this. The connection and depth. Something I hadn't had in forever.

Or ever, really.

"I'm not going anywhere, princess." I loved that nickname for her. It fit. She was a princess to me. I might not be a hero, but I would do anything I could for her. Take care of her. Save her. Support her. Cherish her.

I was falling head over heels for this woman. Hell, if I thought she would accept it, I would tell her now.

Slipping a hand down over her hip, I squeezed. "I like feeling you underneath me just as much. Your body is heaven, Rayne. *You're* heaven."

"I'm not."

Smirking down at her, I kissed her. "I'll be the judge of that."

Our bodies stayed connected, and I couldn't stop touching her. Kissing her. Smoothing my hands over her skin and learning every freckle, every curve. Rayne relaxed beneath me until she was a puddle. When I accidentally bumped her ankle, she whimpered.

Placing my cheek against hers, I spoke softly. "I'm not going anywhere, okay? I want to get you some medicine for your ankle and both of us some food. Then I'll be back."

"Okay," she breathed.

It was almost painful to separate from her. We both shuddered as I pulled out of her body. Then I wrapped her up in the blankets, enjoying the flush on her skin from the fire and her embarrassment over being taken care of.

I understood it. Rayne was someone who took care of everyone else. Her very profession made it mandatory. She would never have to worry about that with me.

Both of us were tired, and I didn't think we wanted to spend time eating something messy. I grabbed us a feast of granola bars and Pop-Tarts, bottles of water and some industrial-strength meds for her foot. I'd been determined to get the wood inside, but I should have given them to her the second I got her undressed and warm.

Before settling with her, I decided we needed more. It was too cold now for us to be in the bed, even with the fire. So we would bring the bed to us. "Let me move you for a second," I said, lifting her into the chair. "I have an idea."

I pushed the couch back, and before I could second-guess myself, I was hauling the mattress off the bed and down the couple of steps in front of the fire. "We'll have to be careful of the blankets, but we'll be warmer."

Rayne looked at me sleepily. "All we need is a blanket fort, and it's a sleepover."

"I could make that happen."

She shook her head. "I'd rather just have you."

Her words drove me faster, piling the rest of the pillows and blankets on the mattress before laying her on it and giving her the medicine.

My last step was to push the couch up against the mattress so we could lean back against it and watch the fire. I pulled Rayne across my chest and settled us beneath the blankets together. Her form softened and her eyes closed, sinking into a drifting doze as I stared at the flames.

We might be absolutely fucked right now, but it was hard to feel that way. Because for the first time in forever, I felt whole.

And happy.

# Chapter 22

**Rayne**

THE BLIZZARD WEAKENED. It wasn't gone, and certainly not over, but you could feel the tipping point in the air. We were snowed in. It was deep enough to make sure we had no choice in making it down the mountain.

Thankfully, Cole had secured supplies for at least a week, and if we needed to, we would break in to Jimmy's stash in the basement.

Up here, we were in our own little world. We tried the satellite phone occasionally, but the storm was still too thick for us to get through. I didn't know the details, but I was sure the blizzard surrounding us was the worst storm Montana had had in at least twenty years. The kind of storm people would be talking about for years.

If it was as bad on the ground as it was in the mountains.

Cole curled his arm around my waist, gently running his other hand through my hair. My back pressed into his chest as

I stared into the flames, and his lips slowly teased my neck and ear.

We'd barely stopped touching each other since we started, and I had no regrets. I'd thought I might, but this felt so right, and we were so far away from the realities of our world, I could just exist in the warmth of his attention.

My ankle felt much better today. The swelling was down, and it was clear it definitely wasn't broken. Still aching and painful, but it wouldn't take too long to recover.

Cole hadn't stopped taking care of me. Food, blankets, sex. I woke up in the middle of the night with his head between my legs, halfway to orgasm, and he didn't stop until I'd found pleasure twice on his tongue.

Now, the way he touched me, it was hard to keep my eyes open. With not much to do but sleep, eat, and have sex, I felt like I was catching up on all the rest I'd skipped in the last few years.

"You asleep, princess?"

"No." I wasn't, and I was glad I faced away from him. His calling me princess made me feel things I couldn't explain. I knew the psychology behind it, and I didn't care. Here and now, I wasn't going to question it.

"Will you talk to me?" Cole brushed his lips across the top of my ear, making goose bumps bloom over my skin.

Slowly, I rolled onto my back so I could see him. "What about?"

"I'm still curious about what you said. About the bad things that happen to the people you love."

My stomach plummeted. I didn't want to think about it, but at the same time, I couldn't exactly argue he hadn't earned the right to know.

"Curious is the wrong word. I'm not *curious* about something that causes you pain. But I would like to know, if you'll tell me."

I looked at him, tracing his face with my eyes. The glow of the fire painted him in oranges and golds. A couple of days' worth of stubble grew on his face, lending him a rugged vibe.

"They're not fun stories."

"No." His eyes crinkled with a smile, but it was a sad one. "I wouldn't imagine so."

Swallowing, I turned toward him. I pressed my face to his chest, unable to look at him while I spoke about it.

"My sister," I said quietly.

Cole brushed his hand up and down my spine with intention. "I didn't know you had a sister."

"I do. Younger. When she was little, we were at the park. The suburbs of Chicago. It was a beautiful place to live. She's seven years younger than me."

"What's her name?"

"Ava."

"That's pretty," he said softly.

Slipping my hand around his back, I held myself closer to him, and he held me right back. "I was supposed to be watching her. But I had some friends there, and so did she. I wasn't paying attention. So it was my fault."

Cole's fingers traced patterns on my skin. No hesitation or slowing down, just waiting for me to speak.

"She climbed a tree. Way too high. Even though she was small, the branches up there wouldn't take her weight. And she fell."

I took one deep breath in and let one deep breath out, remembering it so vividly. "I'll never forget her screams," I said. "On the way down and once she was on the ground."

For a minute, I couldn't speak, the horror and the grief clogging up my throat the way they always did when I went there with the memories. Like I told my clients, recovery wasn't a straight line, and neither was grief. You could feel good for years. Decades, even, and it could come out of nowhere and slam you into the floor.

Grief and guilt changed you on a cellular level, and there was no shame in knowing it and accepting it. It would always hurt. It was how you handled the hurt that was the true test.

"She landed on her tailbone at exactly the wrong angle. Shattered her spine in a way that couldn't be fixed. She's in a wheelchair now, and always will be. And if I just…hadn't been so absorbed in what I was doing, then maybe she wouldn't be disabled for the rest of her life."

Before he could speak, I kept going. "And believe me, I know. I've gone through everything. I know it technically wasn't my fault, and I know holding on to the kind of grief and guilt I feel won't change it. I've approached it from every angle imaginable. Hell, it's the reason I do what I do. But we can't always change how we feel about something, no matter how much we want to."

Cole lifted his hand from my back, tangling his fingers in my hair, and holding me to his chest. "Rayne."

"My father too," I said. "A couple of years later, right around Christmas, I wanted a special kind of candy. This little shop had made them in our neighborhood, and then they moved to a new location that was much farther away. I threw a fit, because it was a tradition, and I loved traditions. Finally, Dad agreed to go get some. He wanted me to be happy, and I was being a little shit." My voice cracked. "It was snowing. Not as hard as this, but hard enough. And…he didn't come back."

"Oh, Rayne."

Tears spilled over my eyes and onto his skin. "He spun out into oncoming traffic. They say he died instantly, which I'm grateful for. But I'm the reason he was out there, Cole. There's no ambiguity about it. He was out there because he loved me, and my selfishness got him killed."

Cole didn't say anything, and I didn't want him to. There

wasn't anything to say that would make me feel better, and there wasn't anything that would relieve the terrible guilt of being responsible not only for the death and injury of your family, but for their grief and loss, too.

Finally, Cole moved, rolling us together so he was on top of me, pressing me down into the mattresses and pillows the way I told him I liked. The compression calmed me and made me feel…safe.

"You said it's been a long time for you. For sex. How long?"

My cheeks heated, and it wasn't from the fire. "I've had plenty of orgasms over the years, Cole. Don't worry."

One corner of his mouth turned up, but his eyes weren't smiling. They were staring at me and seeing far, far too much. "That's not what I asked."

How long? I barely knew. I wasn't really keeping track. Dating hadn't been off the table, and I had dated people on and off over the years, but I'd always bailed out before it got too serious. It was easier that way.

I had a feeling Cole wasn't someone I could bail out on, no matter how easy that might make it.

"I don't know," I told him honestly. "At least a few years."

"And since you've had anything serious?"

He didn't need me to speak to see the answer. Never.

Cole leaned down and kissed my forehead, letting us live in this moment for a little while. "Listen to me." His voice was barely louder than the crackle of the fire. "I'm an asshole with a savior complex. If something happens to me, it will be entirely because of my own idiocy and nothing to do with you. And even if that were the case, which it's not, I'd still choose to be here with you. The only way you can get rid of me now is to tell me point-blank you want me to leave." He smirked. "And I still might try to convince you."

"Why?" I reached up and ran my fingers through his hair.

He was so handsome I didn't want to stop looking at him, but he terrified me too. Somehow this man had cracked open my shell in spite of my trying desperately to keep it closed.

"Why do I want to be with you?"

Slowly, he kissed my cheeks and temples, the tip of my nose and the corner of my lips before pulling my hands away from him and tangling our fingers. "Because your heart calls to mine."

Whatever I had expected him to say, that wasn't it.

"You're beautiful, Rayne. I don't think I'll ever want to stop looking at you. But that's not why I want to be with you. You're kind. You fight for the people you care about, even if it's against someone like me. You hide yourself behind walls you've built because it's easier to exist alone than to risk being hurt again. So you help other people and pretend it's enough. And I know because I'm the same." He took a breath. "I don't know how to explain what it feels like, but I *know* you. I want to take care of you and be the first person you let inside those walls. Even if it's just the two of us, no one deserves to be alone."

My heart stuttered. "I feel like I should make a joke right now because that was so intense."

"No jokes, princess. Just you and me."

"You say that like it's so easy."

"Nope." Cole shook his head. "It's not going to be easy. We both have our shit to deal with, and you, of all people, know people's shit gets in the way of things. But I want this. I want you. So I don't care if it's easy. We'll figure it out and take it slow. Hell, I'll even go to therapy with you, if that's what it takes."

I snorted inelegantly. "Really?"

"Really."

The idea of Cole and me sitting in couples therapy made

me laugh. We'd probably be at each other's throats the way we were at family dinner.

"What happens when we get out of here?"

"Out of this cabin?" he asked. "I'm getting a burger. A giant, hot one I don't have to make myself. Maybe a milkshake. And take a hot shower somewhere. Then take you to bed again and see where we're at with the Chicago situation. After? Hopefully just life."

He was right. It wouldn't be easy, but I did like the fact that it was simple. Straightforward. We would be together, and that was that. The end.

Cole grinned suddenly. "Having you underneath me gives me all kinds of ideas."

"Does it?" I raised one eyebrow. "What kinds of ideas?"

"I think it will be easier to show you than tell you."

Leaning over, he tossed another log onto the fire before yanking the blankets over both our heads and plunging us both into darkness and pleasure.

## Chapter 23

**Cole**

SEEING the nearly clear air outside was strange. Not completely clear, but the wind wasn't howling, and it looked closer to a normal snowy day than the frozen hell that had been swirling around us for the last few days. Trapped in our own little bubble of the fire and sex and the slow, tortured pleasure I loved giving her.

Rayne was asleep in front of the fire, red hair flared out over our pillows like a waterfall. The blanket had slipped down a little, and I saw the bare skin of her neck in the glow of the firelight.

She had clothes on again, much as I disliked the idea. It was warmer.

The daylight was fading, and it was already getting darker outside. We'd been eating the dry goods I'd purchased, but it was time for us to eat some kind of hot meal, even if it was small. I had my coat, scarf, and gloves on, because being this far away from the blankets and fire was still frigid, despite no longer being quite as dangerous.

A chirp caught my attention.

The satellite phone where I left it resting on the table. "No shit," I whispered.

One solitary bar of signal appeared on the screen. It was weak and fluctuated in and out while I was holding it, but better than nothing.

I found Daniel's number and called it.

"He—o?"

"Daniel?" I stepped to the other side of the cabin in the bedroom since it was at a slightly higher altitude.

"Cole?" My name was again choppy, but I could hear him. "Is that you?"

"It's me. First signal we've been able to get in days."

"Hey, it's Cole," Daniel called to whoever was in the background. "Good to hear from you. One more day and we were going to dig our way to you."

I glanced back toward Rayne. She wasn't visible from this angle, but it didn't sound like she'd woken. "Is it bad down there?"

"Probably not as bad as you, but yeah, we're buried. The whole town is buried. We've got walled paths to get to the animals."

Laughing once, I shook my head. "Sounds about right."

"You guys okay?"

"As good as we can be. Rayne's injured. Not seriously, but her ankle's twisted. Generator burned out, so we've been using the firewood. I think I speak for both of us when I say we'd like to get out of here soon. Any progress?"

Daniel made a noncommittal sound. "We've made contact, but they're not moving quickly. Because we were so sparing with the details, they're not inclined to believe us and keep pushing for more information about 'the source'—what we've been calling Rayne."

"Yeah, I don't think so. We're not going to sell Rayne out when she didn't do anything and is the victim. If the Bureau can't get their heads out of their asses long enough to see we're handing them a gift, they can go fuck themselves."

"I told them pretty much the same thing," Daniel said with a chuckle. "Let's just say they weren't big fans."

"They say anything else?"

Jude's voice was now with Daniel's. "Mostly the same bluster with a dose of intimidation," Jude said. It sounded like I was on speaker. "They said now was the time to tell them everything, especially if we had information about the case."

"Tame for them as far as intimidation."

"Oh," Daniel said. "That wasn't the threatening bit. It was when they told us we shouldn't be messing around with this, because the people they're hearing chatter from don't fuck around. So 'whoever' we were contacting them about needed to be careful—or better yet, come forward."

I swore under my breath. "Sounds about right."

"They said they'd get back to us about the other thing, but they haven't yet," Jude called. "That was a couple of days ago. We wanted to talk to you and Rayne and make sure you were okay before reaching out again."

"Of course these people don't fuck around," I said. "They clearly know who Rayne is, after vandalizing her home and office, and they want the flash drive back. Rayne is asleep right now, so I can say I don't think stealing it back is going to be enough now that it's been opened. The alarm, digital flare, whatever it was. It basically painted a target on her back."

Daniel sighed. "Another reason we don't want to identify Rayne. It's Emma and Simon all over again. They'll do whatever they can to make this case. I'll spare you the details of that conversation. But I don't doubt they'd be willing to use both you and Rayne as bait to catch more of them."

Frustration burned in my chest, my free hand clenching into a fist in an attempt to keep from punching the wall. "I'm so fucking sick of it," I said to myself more than to them. "We need help and information, not roadblocks and manipulation. When I joined the Bureau, they were more about helping people than this bullshit. When Rayne and I can get free, we'll see what we can do about getting the flash—"

"*Stop!*" Jude's yell cracked through the phone. "Stop talking right now."

All three of us fell into silence, and I closed my eyes. There it was. The nearly inaudible *click* in the background that gave away everything. We were being listened to, and we'd already talked far too openly.

"Be safe," Daniel said. "Get out when you can."

"Will do."

Sickness roiled in my gut.

We'd brought her out here to keep her safe, and in one conversation, I might have put her in more danger. With the signal being so bad, it was unlikely whoever was tapping could get an exact pinpoint on our location. But the fact that they were still listening at all told me enough. They hadn't given up, still convinced the drive was in the area. Which it was. And now they knew for sure.

I went back to the stove, where the water was now boiling, and focused on making the rest of our food. Noodles and sauce. As basic as it got. I wasn't sure if I'd be able to eat it now, but for Rayne's sake, I needed to try.

She was terrified of something bad happening to me simply because she let herself get close, but I wasn't. I was worried about something happening to her. Before we'd come out here, I'd already been concerned. Now that we'd finally come together?

I would move heaven and earth to keep her safe.

# Chapter 24

**Cole**

I NEVER STAYED ANYWHERE without an escape plan.

As soon as I'd arrived, I'd mapped the possible exits without even thinking about it. Ways to get out of the cabin and down the mountain, both in the truck and on foot.

But those plans didn't account for eighteen inches of snow, another person, or someone who would struggle to walk.

Not to mention, I *had* an escape plan, but this cabin hadn't been chosen for its tactical advantages. It was available and suited my needs well enough. Getting involved with the Chicago mafia and having to save the woman I loved from them hadn't been on my bingo card for my four-month exile.

*The woman I loved.*

My thoughts spoke the words without any hesitation. It seemed a little crazy for something like that to be true. Where I came from, love needed both time to grow and for one to know everything about the other person.

But with Rayne, I didn't *need* to know everything about her.

Did I want to? Yes. I looked forward to peeling back the rose-petal layers of her soul and savoring the softness she only showed to me. But I didn't have a need to know her first. My soul already knew hers, and that was more than enough.

Looking around the cabin, I saw it in a new light. A defensive light. We needed to get ready in case things went badly, but the snow slowed everything down. We had a little time.

Rayne still slept, so I decided to do some of the prep now. With the storm mostly passed, I could make it outside without fear of getting lost. Thank fuck. If anyone had come for us in the middle of the blizzard, we would have been sitting ducks.

Before it was full dark, I needed to get this done.

I took more rope from Jimmy's stash. It was getting low, and I would replace it before I handed the cabin back over to him. Hopefully the man would be pleased that his hideout worked *mostly* as intended. With the exception of the wood-fueled generator.

I grabbed everything I could from his basement and around the cabin that could make noise and carefully strung them together. There was only so much we could do without power, and an early warning system was about as good as we could get.

My snow clothes were thankfully dry, and I got into them as quickly as possible. I was losing light, and the snow would slow them down, but I didn't know how much. If I were coming after someone, even in this weather, I would do it at night.

If it weren't life-and-death, I might laugh at myself. Out in the snow with rope and clanky utensils, stringing things low between trees. At the moment, I was the stereotype of paranoia.

I did what I could, stringing up the noisemakers and clearing away snow from the edges of the cabin for an easy exit. When I pushed back inside, leg aching from the exertion,

Rayne was sitting up, blinking and looking around. The relief on her face was palpable when she saw me. "You went outside?"

"It's not so bad out there now," I said with a smile. I took off my coat and the wet pants and went to her. "Listen, we need to—"

Rayne grabbed the collar of my shirt and pulled me down to her, kissing me, tangling her tongue with mine.

"I made food. Spaghetti."

"Not hungry for that kind of food."

All my blood shifted south, and I groaned. How was I supposed to resist this woman?

I twisted us so she straddled my lap while I leaned up against the couch. That way, her ankle could rest. God, I couldn't wait for us to be able to do everything in my head. I wanted to fuck her against the wall. On the table. Grab both her ankles with my hands and hold them out of the way while I drove into her.

We got her pajama pants far enough off to work, and Rayne reached between us, pulling my cock out of the boxer briefs I still had on. Neither of us could wait any longer than that. She sank down onto me with aching slowness, hands on my shoulders.

"I hope you don't mind," I said. "I've decided I'm going to live with my cock inside you. You're not allowed to go anywhere else. Just sit on me so I can feel you like this."

She laughed breathlessly. "I think both our jobs might object to that."

Pulling her face to mine, I consumed her mouth. "Who needs a job when I can have your pussy?"

"Cole." She ground down onto me, moving her hips in a way that made lights flash behind my eyes.

More. Faster. This wasn't a time for soft and slow. I needed to feel her like I needed to breathe. I grabbed her hips and yanked her down harder on my cock, making sure her clit made contact with every stroke. "That's right, princess. Say my name."

"Cole," she whispered again, head dropping onto my shoulder. She breathed it into my neck. "Cole."

My eyes rolled back in my head as she squeezed down on me like a vise. "You have no idea what hearing my name on your lips does to me, Rayne. It turns me into an animal. A caveman. I want to mark you as mine and mine alone."

I drove up into her, unleashing all that was left of my strength and reaching between us to find her clit. She released a broken cry—the first sign I'd found what she needed. There it was. I loved the sound of her orgasm and the feel of her pulsing around my cock. It was heady and addictive.

*Mine.*

Gripping her hair, I pulled her mouth to mine again, just stopping short of kissing her. "Let me have it, princess. Close your eyes, and give me your pleasure."

Rayne threw her head back, going over the edge, hauling in ragged breaths that told me she was imploding. I wasn't sure which I liked better—the sound of her screaming my name as she came, or this. Silent and breathless and so overcome she *couldn't* make a sound.

Releasing myself, I drove upward. Three more strokes, and I came. With Rayne, I was always halfway there.

When I lifted her off my cock, it shone with her wetness in the firelight. My body was drenched with her, and if I had it my way, I'd spend the rest of my life that way. But right now, I needed to make sure we were both alive in order to stay like that.

"Here," I said, helping her into her pajama pants.

Rayne's eyes were glazed in the aftermath of her orgasm. She laughed quietly. "Getting a girl dressed this fast after sex isn't a great sign, Cole."

I laughed too. "Rayne, if everything was exactly the way I wanted it, we'd spend a month in this cabin. Warm and comfortable, able to go outside if we wanted to, and with nothing better to do than fuck each other for days. You wouldn't be allowed to wear clothes in here, and I'd tie you to the bed just to make sure it happened. Am I clear?"

"Clear." The single word was raw, her eyes wide with shock and lust as she stared at me.

Pulling up my own underwear, I put pants on. "But we need to talk about some things, about this predicament we're in, and I can't be distracted by your body while we do it."

She grinned. "Am I that distracting?"

"One kiss and I needed to stop everything and fuck you. What do you think?"

Rayne sat up and brushed through her hair with her fingers, but I caught the satisfaction there. I'd give her more where that came from. It didn't have to be this cabin. It could be her house. Or an island in Mexico where we could spend time on the beach and take off our suits in the water. I could tie her to beds there too.

I started to harden again before shifting my thoughts. *Get it together, Cole.*

"While you were sleeping, and I made the food—which we'll need to heat up again, by the way."

Rayne winked unapologetically.

"There was a signal on the sat phone. Not much, but I got through to Daniel."

Suddenly Rayne's focus turned on like a laser. "What?"

"Yeah. He caught me up to speed. I have good news and bad news. Which do you want first?"

# Chapter 25

**Rayne**

"I HAVE good news and bad news. Which do you want first?"

I winced. Somewhere deep inside, I had hoped there would be no bad news. "Good news, I guess."

Cole picked me up and once more straddled me across his lap. Exactly the way we'd just been, but with clothes. It made me wish there weren't clothes again.

Suddenly having sex—*real* sex—made me ravenous for it. Cole had just fucked me to an incredible orgasm, and I already wanted more. This was what people talked about when they mentioned the honeymoon phase. An insatiable need for each other that couldn't be denied.

If we had power and infinite supplies, the month in the cabin he mentioned sounded nice.

"Good news is everyone is okay. Daniel said they had walled snow paths to the animals, but the town is just as buried as we are."

"That's the good news?" My stomach plummeted. It was,

but as far as good news went in our situation, not what I was hoping to hear.

"That's the good news."

"I hoped there was more."

He tucked a strand of hair behind my ear, gaze falling to my mouth. "Me too. Daniel got a hold of the FBI, but they're being cagey and aggressive. Pretty much what we expected. They want to know more than we're willing to tell them, given your role in things and how sensitive it is."

Staring at him, I frowned. "Is that the bad news? Because it seems like fairly average news."

Cole's lips firmed into a line, confirming my fear that wasn't all he had to say. "The call was tapped."

"What?"

"Jude caught it, but we don't know how much they heard or what kind of read they got on them. There's a chance they know where we are. That's why I was outside, setting up some early alarm signals just in case. It's not much, but we don't need a lot."

My heart rate spiked, the same fear and panic from the night my house was broken in to washing over me in a tidal wave.

Cole took my face in his hands. "I'm not going to let anything happen to you, Rayne. Do you believe me?"

I did. Cole would do whatever was needed in order to protect us both. Opening my mouth to answer him, I suddenly didn't have a chance.

A broken jangle of clattering metal sounded in the distance. Cole went still. "Get your coat and boots on *now*." He set me on my feet and jumped into the wet jeans he'd abandoned. I wasn't moving as fast as I could without my hurt ankle, but Cole was ready in seconds, helping me get the boot on my injured foot. I groaned at the pressure. "Sorry, princess," he said. "Better than being dead."

I didn't disagree.

He took my face in his hands again. "I'm going to protect you, but this is going to be cold and awful. We'll get through it. Promise. Where's the flash drive?" I pointed over to the desk where I'd sat that first day of the blizzard pretending I didn't desperately want to see him naked. He grabbed it on our way out the back. We were out in the snow less than thirty seconds after hearing the sound. While I'd slept, he'd planned this.

Cole lifted me over another string of kitchen utensils and cups, going around a larger rock and into the deeper snow. From this angle, they wouldn't immediately see our retreating path.

"Where are we going?" I whispered.

He didn't answer, focused on the path in front of us. My ankle screamed, my pulse pounding in it.

The sky still had a tiny touch of light to it, and the reflection off the snow left us able to see, but it was still dark. The snow was so deep it felt like wading through mud. We wouldn't get far.

The dark seemed even darker when we reached an outcropping of rocks that was more free of snow than other parts of the mountain. I could see more pockets like this farther up the hill as the wind had cleared away the snow from the jagged boulders sticking out in the wind.

"Stay here," Cole said, guiding me into the little shadowy hole.

"Cole, *wait*," I hissed, but he was gone, back down the hill. The cabin was still visible through the trees. We weren't far, but Cole was right. We didn't need much; we just needed enough. There was no way for us to run with my ankle like this, and Cole couldn't carry me all the way up the mountain. Or down it.

Shattering glass sounded from down the hill, and seconds later, Cole was back, fitting himself into the small space beside me and pulling me into his arms. "I messed up the snow a bit on the path," he said. "So it's less obvious."

"Still pretty obvious though, right?"

I felt him nod.

A shadow passed through the glimmering firelight in the windows. "Oh god."

They really were there. They'd found us all the way out here. "I didn't think they'd get here this fast," Cole whispered, barely above a breath.

More sounds of destruction, and I leaned closer to him, sharing his warmth. The storm might be over, but it was still after dark in the snow. Cold sank through me, and soon, I was shivering uncontrollably.

"We're going to freeze," I said, barely able to get the words out through my chattering teeth.

"No," Cole said. "We're not. They're going to give up before that. We're going to be okay, Rayne."

His determination would have to be enough for the both of us.

"We should have just let them find it."

"No." Cole's breath tickled my ear. Another ear-splitting crash came from down the hill. "The drive is the only bargaining chip you have. If they take it, they can still assume you've seen it and try to kill you. If you have it, at the very least, you have the power.

"Besides, this asshole *needs* to get taken down. I don't like how the Bureau is going about this, but if these guys can get away with killing people like this, there's no incentive for them to stop."

"Yeah."

I wished doing the right thing felt easier when people were trying to kill you and wouldn't think twice about it.

Voices echoed up from below. "Doesn't look like anything, but they're probably close."

Montana Rain

"No," another one said, echo going faint. "It's been a few hours. Fuckers heard the tap. They're long gone. The guy is FBI, so he's not dumb, unfortunately. We won't find them now, and I'm not about to go searching over an entire mountain in the dark. If they freeze, good riddance. We'll check everywhere around here again, because I don't want to come back. Maybe wait a while and see if they show up."

"Should we torch the place after?"

"I wish." A laugh. "I don't think Antonio wants to get a phone call asking if we can start a fire in fucking Montana. If it spreads? We'd be in deep shit. They care about stuff like that here."

"How can a fire spread with this much snow?" The second voice got fainter and disappeared with the door closing behind him.

"The one good thing about this," Cole said quietly, "is that they'll leave a path. They have no reason to hide their trail. We might be able to get out of here. But we need to wait until we're absolutely sure they're gone and far enough away that we won't run into them."

I nodded.

If they were going to wait around inside, we couldn't move. All we could do now was hope we didn't freeze before they left.

Cole turned me toward him and held me against his body. It wasn't the same as huddling under blankets, but it was better than nothing. The outcropping hid us from the wind. Otherwise, we'd be screwed.

"You never told me what you wanted to do when you get out of here," he whispered, breath warming my cheek.

"I don't know."

"Sure you do," he teased. "Tell me."

My voice was muffled by the way we were pressed together. "I agree with you about the food, but I want pizza. A giant fucking pizza. Or a big bowl of ravioli. And I want a bath. A

171

long one that I can just soak in for a while and forget about ever being cold."

"Is there room for me in this bath?" he asked.

"Maybe," I sighed. "But it's not a sex bath. This is a relaxation bath, and they're entirely different."

He laughed quietly. "Noted, princess."

I closed my eyes and let him hold me, focusing on images of warmth and heat in order to fight off the cold. Thinking about how much time was passing only made it worse, so I didn't think about that. I imagined the steaming hot bath I would take and the big, cheesy bowl of pasta I wanted.

Cole held me close, shifting us so he was on the outside of our hideout, shielding me from any kind of wind. But it wasn't enough for either of us. The cold slowly sank through my clothes and into my skin. My teeth chattered uncontrollably, and I started to feel sleepy. How long had we been out here?

"I'm going to go look," Cole said. "Hang on, Rayne."

He moved, and it got colder. I couldn't respond or move to tell him no or to be careful. All concept of time had disappeared, so I had no idea how long he was gone. Only that it was torture without him.

"We're clear," Cole said, head appearing over the rocks. "Come on, let's get you out of here."

Reaching beneath me, he scooped me up and began to carry me down the hill. "I can—"

"You're freezing, and we're not running. I can carry you."

I buried my face deeper in his chest. "You're cold too."

"I am," he agreed. "We're both going to be warmer soon."

The inside of the cabin was destroyed, just like my house and office had been. A total mess. This time, though, there *were* holes torn in the couch and mattress, looking for hiding places.

"Anything you need?" Cole said. "From here?"

My clothes and his were strewn across the room, and I

shook my head. Nothing that I couldn't live without. I hadn't even brought my laptop. "My phone."

I'd stuck it beneath the couch from when we were sleeping, and it was still there. Cole found his as well, though I noticed the screen was shattered. "Let's see if we can get out of here, okay?" he said. "No point in staying here when they already know where the cabin is. We'll be safer at the ranch for now."

Safer *and* warmer.

Cole set me down on the ruined couch. "Hold tight, princess."

My mind didn't seem to be fully working. What little remained of the fire helped, but I was still so cold, the temptation to close my eyes and rest was overwhelming. Now I knew why it was so easy for people to freeze to death.

Outside, an engine turned over and failed. Again. Again. The sound became part of the background. Until finally, there was the roar of the truck coming to life. The door to the cabin opened, and I cringed against the cold it let in.

"We got lucky, Rayne. Got the engine warmed up enough to work, and there's a path from the others coming up here. Not much of one, but it's enough."

He lifted me up again, and this time, I didn't protest. The inside of the truck's cab was already warm when he set me inside, and it was perfect. Cole kept me close, tucking me in beside him as he slowly worked the truck around in the snow to face down the mountain.

"Hold on," he said. "We're not out of this yet."

No, we weren't, but I was with Cole, so as I closed my eyes and dozed, I knew we would be all right.

# Chapter 26

**Cole**

"SHIT," Rayne hissed out the word. The steam coming off the water in the large tub was an indication of how hot it was. Probably too hot for both of us, but we needed it.

I wasn't totally sure how we'd made it down the mountain, but we had, and we'd gotten to the ranch. Daniel and the others jumped into action, bundling us into the Clark Fork cabin. Evie was bringing clothes for Rayne, and Lucas for me. They would drop off both clothes and food in the main area of the cabin while Rayne and I got warm.

To everyone's credit, they said nothing about Rayne and me getting into the bath together. And, to be fair, banishing whatever remained of the cold from us was more important than anything else.

The truck had been warm, but Rayne had been out in the cold nearly too long. Her energy was coming back now, but the feeling of scalding heat against pure cold wasn't fun. "I know,"

I said, helping her down into the water before stepping in behind her. "Fuck."

It burned. But it also felt incredible.

Sliding down, I gritted my teeth as I fit Rayne to my chest, wrapping my arms around her. We were off the mountain and relatively safe. It wasn't perfect by any means, and as soon as we were warm, I was sure Jude, Daniel, and the others would want to talk to us about it. But Rayne came first.

I grabbed her hands and intertwined our fingers, holding them under the water. She groaned, and I kissed her neck. "I've got you."

"This is a bitch," she said through her teeth.

"Yes, it is."

Outside the bathroom, I heard the front door open and low speech before it closed again.

Neither Rayne nor I said much, just sinking deeper into the water until she had turned and was sprawled across my chest, and we breathed more easily. "Sorry I hijacked your bath," I said quietly.

"I'm not."

"You ready to get out?"

She mumbled the words into my skin. "No, but I'm also hungry."

"The food should be here."

I helped her out of the tub, and it was glorious to have the air in this cabin be warm. Clothes and a whole bag of food had been placed on the kitchen table.

"I won't lie," I said. "I don't want you to put your clothes on."

The simple pajamas Evie had brought Rayne didn't change the fact that she'd just been naked and wet in my arms. She blushed, twisting her damp hair up off her neck. "I'm sure you'll take them off later."

A strange type of relief went through me. I crossed the

room and took her face in my hands, kissing her breathless. "Part of me was afraid we'd come back to real life and you'd change your mind."

"I think it's a little late for that," she whispered. "You cracked my shell."

I grinned. "Damn right, I did."

Rayne peeked in the bags and gasped. "You had them bring ravioli?"

"I mentioned it's what you'd wanted, but I also said that food itself was more important."

A container of pasta for each of us was in the bag, and the sounds coming out of Rayne's mouth made it more than worth it to delay my burger craving. They also made me so hard I could barely see straight.

After we ate our fill, I texted Daniel that we were ready. It was late now, but they came straight over. Rayne and I were in the living room, sitting separately, much to my annoyance, when they came in.

"Glad you both are safe."

"It was touch and go there for a bit," I admitted.

Jude sat down and leaned his elbows on his knees. "It's been an eventful night for everyone."

Rayne looked at him. "Oh?"

"We gave the FBI *some* of what they wanted," he said. "We told them we had a drive with information integral to their case. We also told them that due to the contents and the offensive nature of the virus, we couldn't risk sending the information digitally, nor were we comfortable sending it through the mail. Not least because you need it, Rayne."

"Can't imagine they were happy with that," I said sarcastically.

"No," Daniel said. "But they want the drive, and they want the *source*—" he nodded to Rayne "—in Chicago to be interviewed and make sure you don't know anything else. They know nothing else about you other than you came into contact with the drive in a way that was completely unintentional and are now a target."

Rayne pulled her knees up to her chest. "You think I should go?"

The question wasn't directed at Daniel and Jude. She looked straight at me. "It doesn't mitigate all the risk," I told her. "But handing the Justice Department ammo against these guys is a good thing, and they'll protect you."

"If I don't go, then this is never over," she pointed out. "At least if I give them the drive, it's off the table."

I nodded. "They're trying to prevent anyone from knowing what's on there. If the FBI already knows, there's not really a point to taking out everyone who could say something. I won't lie to you. It doesn't mean they won't still try, but I agree it's your best option right now."

Daniel shifted. "They have arrangements in place to get you there quickly and anonymously. All we have to do is tell them, and you'll be on a flight tomorrow."

"Cole too," Rayne said.

The tightness in my chest eased. I wanted to go with her, though I didn't have any right. But watching her walk out of my sight when someone was *hunting* her? Unthinkable.

Jude looked at me. "Think your pals will be okay with you tagging along?"

"They better be," I said. "Because I'll be there either way."

Rayne's eyes were on mine, and mine were on hers. Out of the corner of my eye, I saw Daniel and Jude look between the two of us, clearly seeing what we no longer hid. "Thanks," she said.

"Make the call," I told them. "We'll be ready whenever they are."

"Will do," Jude said, standing.

Daniel stood as well. "You guys are good *here*?" The single word told me he'd been planning to offer one of us a different cabin. He watched Rayne, waiting for the answer, as it should be.

Her cheeks turned pink, and she pressed her lips together. "Yeah, we're okay. Thank you."

"Keep your phones on," he said with a nod. "We'll let you know the plan as soon as we're able."

"Thank you."

I saw them to the door, locking it behind them.

"You really want to come with me?"

Raising an eyebrow, I strode toward her and lifted her off the couch. "I'm glad you asked first, because I know it's probably an asshole move, but letting you walk away from me to go to the city where the mafia is hunting you alone? That was never going to happen."

"You're right," she said. "It is a bit of an asshole move. But in this case, I don't mind."

The air in the bedroom felt good after being chilled in the other cabin for so long. "Sex when we're already warm? Maybe I'll get a chance to overheat you."

Rayne laughed, already pulling herself up closer to me. "So sure we're having sex?"

"Only if you want," I said mildly, my body hardening as she brushed her lips over my neck. "But I've only just started on the list of ways I need to make you come."

She pulled back, staring at me as I lowered her to the bed and flicked on the low lamp. "There's a list?"

"There is." I lowered myself over her. "It's a very long list."

Rayne's eyes sparkled, the fierceness I loved back in her gaze. "I guess we better get started, then."

CHICAGO FELT DIFFERENT NOW.

While I hadn't been happy here because it represented my failure, now it felt like a battlefield. Even being escorted from the plane directly to the field office felt risky. Rayne felt the same, keeping her hand in mine, and I didn't care that she squeezed my hand so tight it left marks.

The Bureau had put us on a plane under false names, and passing through security was easier than I'd imagined it would be. But we were here now, pulling up to the field office through the downtown streets.

Without even discussing it, both of us felt more at ease around each other and showing what we were to others. Now, in the back of the car, I held Rayne against me, my lips at her temple, and she held me where she could. If she needed an anchor, I would happily be there for her.

Rayne kept reaching her hand into her inner coat pocket where the flash drive was kept, making sure it was still there. I understood the impulse, but we were almost there.

"Thank you for coming with me," she whispered. Even though she was quiet, the guy driving us looked back in the rearview mirror. I glared at him, and he looked away.

"Do I say the sweet thing or the funny and asshole-sounding but true thing?"

I felt the quiet vibration of her laugh. "Both."

My sentiment last night had been the same and perfectly clear. "The funny thing, then—it's funny you think you had a choice about my coming. I would have come either way."

She slapped my stomach, but it wasn't hard. "And the other one?"

Reaching up, I cupped her face with one hand, hiding my mouth behind her ear so the driver couldn't read my lips. "You never have to thank me for supporting you, Rayne. It's all I want."

She shook, fingers digging into my shirt. "I'll still thank you."

"We're almost there," I told her. "Then we'll get you back to your life, and me to my exile, and see where we go from there."

The car pulled up to the curb, a group of agents in suits ready to greet us. I got out of the car first, looking around even though we were surrounded by the Bureau. After everything last year, I wasn't taking any chances.

Taking Rayne's hand, I pulled her out of the car, and they ushered us inside.

A whirlwind of activity surrounded Rayne. Paperwork— always so much fucking paperwork—and passing over the flash drive. And finally, they ushered her into an interview room to ask her about everything that had happened so far.

My interview was much shorter, so she was still in the room when I got out, and they let me into the room behind the one-way glass.

The door opened, and Special Agent Bordeaux came in. While I was here, he'd been my supervisor's supervisor's supervisor. I nodded to him.

"You did good on this one, Phillips."

"I didn't do anything," I said.

He chuckled. "Don't sell yourself short. You protected an asset and got vital evidence to us in time to make a difference. And you did it when you didn't have any reason to help the Bureau, so thank you."

I kept my mouth shut, tempted to tell him that having a reason to help the Bureau shouldn't matter when you were doing the right thing, but I didn't. It wouldn't be useful right now.

"Anyway," he said. "This puts you in the clear. You already were, but this contribution will drive any shadows of doubt from people's minds."

Looking over at him, I tried to see if he was serious. It seemed like he was. "Really?"

"Yeah. When you suggested the leave, brass thought it was good for you to take some time, more for everyone else than for you. Keep you out of sight so the taint of association would fade. But with this? You're good. If you want to come off administrative leave early and go back into the field, you can. I'll even see what I can do about a transfer back to Seattle, though we'd love to keep you here."

"Wow," I said. "Thank you."

He looked at me expectantly, and I didn't know how to interpret what I was feeling. Bordeaux offered everything I wanted. Everything I *thought* I wanted. But his telling me I could come back and dive back into work didn't have the shine and sparkle I'd thought it would.

Maybe I was tired from everything that had happened the last few days. Maybe I was disillusioned about what this job actually was. But the truth of my thoughts told me I wasn't sure the Bureau was where I wanted to be now.

"Would there be any objections to me staying on the admin leave? I have some things I need to see through."

Bordeaux shrugged. "No, we've already made arrangements for it, and that gives us plenty of time to get you set up wherever you want to be."

I reached out and shook his hand. "I'll think about it and let you know."

"Do that. And thank you, seriously." He clapped me on the shoulder before leaving the room, and I looked back at Rayne, where she was finishing up her interview. A month ago, I would have said that conversation was a dream come true.

Now? Now I thought I might have found some better dreams.

# Chapter 27

**Rayne**

"I THINK that's all we need from you," the special agent across the table from me said. She was organizing her papers. "You've been very helpful."

"I'm glad."

She smiled. "We spoke about protection, and while you're in Chicago, we can position agents at your hotel to accompany you places. You can keep your driver. But we don't believe witness protection is necessary. If it had escalated further, maybe it would be different. But at this point, you don't qualify. You didn't witness a crime, and you're no longer in possession of anything worth taking back.

"By that measure, and based on chatter and our sources, you're safe and in the clear."

"Thank you," I said. Though I would have done witness protection if it were truly necessary, it was my worst nightmare. Who wanted to be completely uprooted from their life, never to speak to anyone again unless a trial went the way they needed? Even then, it wasn't a guarantee.

I didn't want to leave everything behind. Especially now. "If something comes up?"

"We'll let you know," she assured me. "We're very aware of the situation."

"Thank you," I said again as she stood.

Cole waited for me outside the door, and he didn't hesitate to draw me into his arms. My ankle was okay, but leaning against him was easier. If I asked him, he'd carry me in a heartbeat.

"Feel better?" he asked.

"Not sure. I don't think it's sunk in yet."

"I get that. Hotel? Food?"

I sighed. "Yeah."

The Bureau had booked that for us too. Though not the same hotel where I'd gotten the flash drive. It had been a long day. Anytime you flew out of Montana, it was a long day. I was tired, but I still needed to do something.

Cole carried the small suitcases we'd cobbled together into the single hotel room. We'd only asked for one, and I didn't mind. If they'd gotten us two, we probably would have only used one anyway.

"Think I can get the Bureau to pay for room service? Or I'll order you the Thai food you wanted," he offered with a grin.

"Can I ask you something?"

His face dropped into seriousness. "Are you okay?"

"Yeah, I'm fine. Tired, but fine."

Cole tipped my face back and kissed me. "Good."

"I need to go see my mom and sister," I said quietly. "And I want you to meet them, but I also don't think I can show up with you out of the blue."

He smiled, and I saw understanding in his eyes. "You want to prep your family for me?"

"Yes." I blushed. "Going from no one for years to you—and you being an FBI agent, along with why I'm here in Chicago—might be a little much if I arrive with you in tow."

"Princess, that's going to be a lot, regardless. How much are you going to tell them?"

Leaning against him, I let my forehead fall on his chest. "Enough for them to understand the seriousness. Not enough to make them scared."

"Good. And good luck with balancing that, by the way."

I groaned, and he laughed. "Do you want to eat first?"

"No. I want to go and come back, then eat. And sleep."

Cole brushed my hair back from my face. "Okay. Take the agent with you. Better yet, let's see if they'll drive you over."

"Good idea."

He pulled out his phone, and I put my suitcase on the bed, digging through the borrowed clothes. No one had thought it was a good idea for me to go back to my house while I was still in possession of the flash drive. I owed Evie the biggest bouquet of flowers ever. And a cake. And a gift card.

I slipped into fresh jeans and a T-shirt, making a note to shower when I came back to get the rest of the plane off me. Cole slipped an arm around my waist and put his chin on my shoulder. "They're coming up to the door."

How did we get here? The casual affection he showed felt *right*, yet just days ago, I'd resisted it so hard I'd been sure it would never happen.

Nerves tumbled in my gut.

The old fear surfaced and gripped me like a closing fist. It gave me the urge to push him away and tell him he shouldn't be so close. But I didn't want to. I wanted to stay here where it felt safe.

"I want to meet them," Cole said. "When you're ready for it."

"I want to meet your family too."

His arm around my waist squeezed me gently. "My parents passed a few years ago, and you know about my brother. It's just me now."

"I'm sorry."

Cole kissed the side of my neck, that fire he always seemed to infuse into my veins spreading quickly. "I'm all right," he said. "Now stop procrastinating. And be careful of your ankle."

"Don't tell me what to do."

"I think you like it when I do." His lips curved against my ear.

Stepping away from him, I made a face. "I think you're trying to provoke me."

"You're right. Because now I can get you riled up and kiss you to calm you down, and it's the best of both worlds."

A knock sounded on the door, and I rolled my eyes. "Keep dreaming, Cole."

"Only of you, princess."

The agent didn't say much, accompanying me to the car. It was the same driver we'd had on the way from the airport and between the field office and the hotel. All he needed to know was the address of my mom's apartment.

I probably should have called or texted to let them know, but I wanted the surprise. Hopefully, it would be a good one.

"I won't be too long," I said.

"Take your time," the agent said, turning and handing me a card. "I'm here for you, but I'm not going to sit out front in the car for obvious reasons. I'll be around."

Nodding, I put the card in my pocket. "Thanks."

The short walk from the car to the door of the building gave me chills. Like someone had eyes on me, even though I knew better. How long would it feel like this? Looking over my shoulder for someone who wasn't there? Especially now, while I was limping.

I knew the codes to the building and the apartment, so I let myself in the main door. But I knocked on their apartment door. Inside, I heard talking and then footsteps. "Coming!"

A few seconds later, my mom opened the door, her face going slack with shock. "Rayne?"

"Surprise."

"What are you doing here?" She pulled me into a hug that was far more genuine than I'd hoped for.

"Mom, who is it?"

Mom stepped aside, revealing me. "Hey there."

"Oh my god, *what?*"

I laughed. "I found myself in Chicago, and you know I couldn't be here and not come see you."

"You *found yourself* in Chicago?" my mom asked while I leaned down and hugged Ava.

"Yup."

Ava narrowed her eyes. "That doesn't sound suspicious at all."

"I'll tell you in a second. I'm not interrupting anything, am I?"

"No." Mom gestured to the living room. "We're just about to eat dinner. Do you want some?"

"I'm okay." I rested my hand on my stomach. All day, I hadn't been hungry. It would hit me later, I was sure. "Thank you, though."

"Okay." Ava wheeled herself back to the special table that fit over her chair. "Spill the details. Why are you here?"

I laughed, sitting in a chair where I could see them both. "You guys act like it's some kind of miracle I'm here."

Mom gave me a look. "Well, it is. A little."

Making a note to make sure I saw and called them enough

that they didn't act like I was a ghost, I sighed. "I wish it were better news. Do you remember last time, when I came home from the hotel and told you there was a woman being chased?"

"Yes," my mother said. "Why?"

"She wasn't all right. She was murdered."

Ava gasped. Mom looked pale, and I told them the story of what had happened, playing down the dangerous details as much as I could. I also avoided telling them about Cole's involvement, as he would come in at the end.

"So, I'm here. I gave the drive to the FBI, and, in theory, I'm all clear. Though I can't say I'll be sleeping through the night for a while."

Mom shook her head. "God, Rayne. I'm sorry for making you feel bad about being here."

"No," I said. "That's on me. I shouldn't make you guys feel like I'm not a presence in your lives. It's my fault."

Ava rolled her eyes. "Yeah, Rayne? Do us all a favor and don't take on another thing you think is your fault. It's not, and it's exhausting. We love you, we want to see you more, and while we understand why you feel the way you do, *we don't feel that way.*"

I gaped at my sister, shocked at her words, necessary as they were. "I—"

"I know you think that this is your fault." She gestured to her chair. "I know you think Dad is your fault too."

When I glanced at my mother, she nodded. "And you know life doesn't work that way. So, can we all please stop pretending like you have to keep your distance in this messed-up version of you trying to keep us safe? I'd rather just see you."

Tears filled my eyes, along with shame I'd work through later. "I'm sorry, squirt. I should know better."

"I'm in therapy too," Ava said. "So is Mom. Therapists have problems, Rayne. Everyone has problems. But I'm done ignoring the wheelchair-shaped elephant in the room."

I laughed in spite of myself, tears running down my face. "I really am sorry. I'm still working on it, I promise."

"We know," Mom said. "We can tell. Still."

Taking one deep breath in and letting it out, I bowed my head. "I'm hearing you loud and clear."

"Good. I expect you to keep up your end of it, though. I'll call your ass out on avoidance."

Looking at my sister, I appreciated the young woman she'd turned into. There was nothing stopping her, including her disability—and including me. "You got it. I actually have something else to tell you along those same lines," I said. "I met someone, and as hard as I tried to push him away, he got through. He's here with me, and I would love for you to meet him. I left him at the hotel because I didn't want to spring the 'Mafia coming after me' thing and a guy at the same time."

Ava's face lit up. "Oh my god, *yes*. It's about fucking time."

"Language," Mom said, and Ava ignored her.

"What's his name? What does he do? When can we meet him?"

Wiping away what remained of the tears, I smiled. "His name is Cole. He's an FBI agent, though this isn't the way I met him, and if you want to, you can meet him tomorrow."

"*Yes.*"

I looked over at my mother. "Is that okay? What's your schedule like?"

She smiled, and it felt like one of the first times I'd seen *true* happiness in her eyes. Or maybe it had always been there, and I was the one who'd been dimming the shine. "Don't worry about my schedule. We'd love to meet him. I get the feeling our meeting him is important?"

My heart stuttered in my chest. "Yeah."

"Lunch?" Ava asked. "We can order Rudy's."

Rudy's was one of our favorite places from when I still

lived here. They had everything from sandwiches to pasta. "That sounds amazing."

"He's here at the hotel?" Mom asked. "Alone?"

I nodded.

Ava wheeled herself backward and turned for the door. "What are you doing here, then? Go and bring him back tomorrow."

"I can stay longer. He's a big boy."

"Rayne." My sister stared at me. "You're not nearly as mysterious as you think you are, and you haven't been with anyone serious in forever. Better believe I'm going to do everything I can to encourage this."

My mother was holding in her laughter, and I was too. Ava hadn't yet decided what she wanted to do, if anything. But whatever it was? She'd be an absolute powerhouse.

Leaning down, I kissed her head. "Okay. We'll be here at noon for lunch."

"I'm counting down from thirty for you to get out the door."

Laughing, I pulled out my phone and texted the driver before waving goodbye. She'd put a smile on my face in spite of my exhaustion. I loved my family. The trip back to the hotel felt like nothing, and Cole saw the difference. "Good visit?"

"Yes. We're going over for lunch tomorrow."

"Perfect."

I peeled the T-shirt over my head. "I desperately need a shower. I still feel like I have plane stuck to me."

"Want some company?" He raised an eyebrow.

Just the thought of Cole naked and wet had me flushing red. I wasn't used to this. If I knew anything to be true, it was that Cole had proven himself to be so far from the man I'd thought he was. This was the man who'd existed beneath, instead of the one driven by pain and fear that had smacked him in the face and made him realize some things.

Similar to the way my sister had just verbally slapped me. It was necessary, and relief sang in my chest. "I would love some."

He was already pulling his shirt over his head in that guy way where he grabbed the back and pulled it straight forward. Cole grinned when he caught me staring. "Do I need to carry you in there? How's your ankle?"

"It's okay," I said truthfully. "It hurts, but it's not too bad."

I stripped off my pants, but Cole caught me before I could get all the way naked. "I think I'm going to have to examine it for myself. Along with some other parts of you that need attention."

He hoisted me over his shoulder. "*Cole*, oh my god. Put me down."

He curled his hand around the back of my thigh, so, so close to the promised land. "In a minute."

I remained over his shoulder while he turned on the water before gently setting me down and stripping me the rest of the way. "I can take my own clothes off, you know."

"And deprive me of the pleasure? I don't think so, princess."

"Princess" was growing on me. Something about the darkness in his voice when he said it made me shiver.

The hotel shower was big and open, with a rainfall shower-head. Most of the time I hated these—they weren't practical for washing your hair, and you had to be cold if you didn't want water in your eyes because you had to step out from underneath them. But something about standing underneath the flow with Cole was incredible.

And just like the fantasy every woman had about getting kissed in the rain, Cole made every inch of that dream come true, hauling my body against his and holding me there with one hand on my ass, the other behind my neck, his cock hard and hot between us.

"Now that I have you out of that cabin, princess, anything can happen."

He'd made good on his promise last night, but I didn't doubt he had more to give. I didn't doubt anything when it came to Cole Phillips. The fact that I could have that thought in my head was, in itself, incredible.

"Gotta check your ankle," he said, voice nearly inaudible in the water. Cole sank to his knees, gently lifting my foot and feeling with his fingers. It wasn't so bad now. The swelling was down, and as long as I took ibuprofen, it was okay. It would be good as new in a few days. I was just lucky I hadn't sprained it or done something worse.

"Looks good." Cole set my foot down gently and slipped his hands around the backs of my thighs. "But since I'm down here."

My hands fell to his shoulders as he pulled my legs apart, pressing his lips to my center. "Cole—"

He hummed against my skin, freezing any protest I had. The hold he had on me—I wasn't going to fall, and he wasn't going to stop.

I didn't want him to.

Cole worshipped me with his mouth and tongue, lifting his hands to squeeze my ass and hold me against him. Already he'd learned what worked for me. The pressure and rhythm that made heat rise beneath my skin and my breath go short.

But I still wasn't fast. "We can move to the bed." I angled my head back, savoring being caught between Cole and the heat of the shower. "You can't be comfortable on your knees."

He moved me, turning me so I leaned against the wall. "If you're thinking about my knees right now, I'm not doing a good enough job." Cole dove in again, not giving me the chance to think or question. The only thing I could do was relax into the bliss of his mouth and cover my own with my hand when the pleasure came barreling out of nowhere, hotter than the shower itself.

"There it is." He gave another long, slow lick between my legs. "You're addictive."

My knees felt weak, and Cole kept my body between him and the wall as he stood, making sure I didn't fall. I let him hold me up as he reached for the hotel shampoo and washed my hair for me.

My skin tingled with chills, reacting to the sensation of Cole's fingers in my hair. God, I loved the feeling of it. He was tall enough to do it too, turning me to face the wall while he finished the job and rinsed my hair before washing my body.

Thoroughly.

The whole time, he hadn't stopped touching me. But now? I needed him to let me go. Grabbing his hand, I smirked at him. "Don't let me fall."

"What—"

I sank down, and Cole went quiet, realizing what I was doing. His mouth opened, and I reached out, placing a hand on his abs. "If you can do it?"

Warmth and humor filled his gaze. "The last time you said that, you hurt your ankle."

"I don't think my ankles are in danger from a blow job."

"I'm sure I could find a way to make it—*fuck*." His voice cut off when my lips met his skin. One hand fell against the shower wall, and the other to my hair. His fingers gripped like he wanted to take control, but he didn't.

It had been forever since I'd done this. And even when I had, I hadn't felt very good at it. Cole's reaction made pleasure curl in my gut. His breath hissed through his lips like he was holding everything back.

I took him into my mouth, closed my eyes, and let instinct guide me. Deeper, enjoying the rhythm of his hips and the friction of his length on my tongue. I wanted to learn him the way he was learning me. Which ways my mouth could make his breath hitch and muscles tense.

"Rayne." Cole's voice was nearly strangled. "I need to be inside you."

Raising an eyebrow, I pulled back. "Fair is fair."

Grasping me beneath the elbows, he lifted me to my feet and shut off the water then picked me up, grabbing a towel on the way out of the bathroom.

He spread me out on the towel and hovered over me, taking my mouth in a bruising kiss. "Is this all right?" he asked, gripping my hips. "I love your mouth, but I need this."

"As long as it wasn't because you didn't like it." I said it lightly, like I was teasing, but I needed to know.

"Absolutely not. It's because I was about to come too soon like a teenager, and like hell do I want the evening to be over before it starts."

"Why, Cole Phillips." I couldn't wipe the smile off my face. "Are you saying you don't have enough stamina to go more than once?"

Cole growled. He *growled*, and I didn't think I'd ever heard something so hot. "You want to test the theory, princess?"

"Maybe."

Spreading my legs, he slid into me in one long, hard thrust, stealing both our breath. Cole grabbed the headboard, and he didn't hold back, driving into me hard and fast. The rest of the water from our shower dripped off him as he stared down at me with singular focus. There was nothing he didn't see. All of me. Every gasp and movement as I reached for him.

Dropping himself down to me, he buried his face in my neck and groaned. "I'll never have enough of you."

"I—"

Light flared behind my eyes, cutting off my words. I came, shuddering around him, and he didn't stop and didn't slow, driving me through one orgasm and taking the opportunity to drive me into another one. "You're going to kill me," I gasped.

"We can't have that. But I want you to give me one more."

"I can't."

"Yes, you can, princess." A kiss brushed across my lips. My forehead. My cheek. Cole rolled his hips, creating the perfect friction, and he was right. I could give him one more. Earth-shattering and body-numbing. I couldn't see or breathe, only knowing pleasure that built on itself, never releasing me.

Somewhere outside of myself, Cole came too, finding his release with shuddering groans before he slowed, giving me his weight but not pulling away.

"Too many," I murmured.

"No such thing. You'll get to more. We just need to practice."

A laugh burst out of me, and I wrapped my arms around his neck. Pushing aside any worry I had, I embraced what my sister had said. Everything was fine. This was fine. I was allowed to be happy, and Cole made me happy.

Pulling him down to kiss me, I didn't fight my smile. "I think I'm going to like practicing."

# Chapter 28

**Rayne**

THE DRIVER DROPPED us off outside the apartment building, Cole helping me out of the car. "Your foot okay?"

"It's good."

"Let me know if it's not."

I glared at him. "You're not carrying me through the streets of Chicago, Cole."

"That's debatable," he muttered, but it was with a smile.

It was strange being here two days in a row. They were right. I needed to be here more often. "Do you guys have your orders picked out?" I asked, pushing open the door. "I need examples so we can show Cole how great Rudy's is."

My words ended in a gasp. The apartment was trashed, and the silence told me no one was inside. "Oh my god."

Cole pulled me behind him. "Hold on," he said.

He went in first, clearing the space room by room before letting me come in. "There's no one."

In the living room, only one piece of furniture was

untouched. The coffee table. A cell phone sat in the center of it, clearly alien in comparison to the rest of the apartment. "Cole."

I picked up the phone, and the screen told me there was a voice mail. Panic tore through my body. Any sense of safety I'd found had vanished the second the apartment door opened.

I was in Cole's arms before I knew what was happening. He took the phone from me and pressed the button so we could both listen.

"It seems we didn't get the message across the first couple of…close calls we had," the voice on the recording said. "If you want to see your mother and sister again, you'll bring the flash drive. And if you don't want anything to happen to them, neither you nor your boyfriend will involve the FBI. Understood? Bring it by five p.m." The voice rattled off an address where we were meant to bring it.

"And don't think this is one of those times when you can go behind our backs. We're watching."

The line went dead, and my breath came in harsh gasps. "Oh god. Oh god." Blinding terror gripped me, not letting me move or breathe. "Cole, they're going to die. I did this, and they're going to die."

My mind spiraled down onto itself. Bad things happened to people who loved me. I'd thought it would be Cole, but it wasn't. It was Mom and Ava. *Again*. I'd done this.

Tears spilled over. I couldn't breathe. "I ruined her life, and now I'm going to be the reason she dies. I can't live with that, Cole. I can't live with it."

His lips landed on mine, his hands holding my face, short-circuiting the panic. "Breathe, princess. They're going to be okay. We're going to get them back. They'll be fine. You didn't do this."

"How can we do anything?" My voice echoed off the walls. "We—"

Covering my mouth with his hand, Cole pulled me out of the apartment and closed the door behind me. My heart beat so fast I thought I might pass out. We went down to the lobby, and only then did he circle me in his arms again. "They could be listening, and we can't give anything away now, okay? Tell me. Tell me what you were going to say."

"We don't have the flash drive anymore," I sobbed. "It's not possible to get a copy from the Bureau. They're going to kill them, and Mom and Ava— they don't have anything to do with it."

Cole crushed me to his chest. "I need you to breathe, Rayne. Everything you're feeling is valid. This is scary. But we can't help them like this."

"We can't help them at all." I clung to him like the lifeline he was.

"That might not be true." I felt him move and heard the click of his new phone unlocking. "I have an idea. More of a hunch. Let's see if I'm right."

The phone rang on speaker, and suddenly, Jude's voice was loud in the echoey space. Cole moved us to a corner where we weren't broadcasting to the world. "Phillips?"

"We have a situation," Cole said.

A long silence extended on the other end of the line before Jude spoke again. "We're encrypted now. Talk to me."

"Rayne's mother and sister have been taken." Jude swore in the background, and I thought I heard the voices of the others too. "They've demanded the flash drive and no FBI involvement."

"But they didn't restrict other involvement?" Jude asked.

"They did not. Which is why I have to ask. Do you have a copy of the files? I saw you messing with the drive after the beacon, and I know damn well you have the skills to undo the flare and the virus. So, I'm asking now if you did it as a backup of a backup plan?"

Another long silence came from the phone. I found myself gripping Cole's shirt while I waited for the answer.

"I do have a copy," Jude said. "It didn't work completely. By disabling the transmitter and the virus, I couldn't save all the contents. But I have enough that a bait and switch might work."

"Jude," I said, aware of the tears in my voice. "Thank you."

Cole pulled me closer. "What do you need from us?"

"If they're watching you, you need to be careful. Is there a business center at the hotel?"

"Yes."

"They can't know you're making a new copy," Jude said. "Because if they realize you've already turned over the flash drive, all your leverage goes out the window."

Cole nodded. "Right. We can't guarantee they don't have eyes inside the hotel."

"No," Daniel said, finally making his appearance known. "We can't be sure of that, but we can take care of it."

"How?"

A low discussion took place on the other end of the line. "Did they give you a deadline?"

"Five p.m. Today. I'm getting the idea that sooner is better."

"Contact?"

"No."

I swallowed, head spinning. This was moving so fast, and all I could think about was whether Mom and Ava were okay. Were they in pain? Were they being tortured? Hopefully not since we hadn't told them no.

"Assume they'll be in touch," Daniel said, and Cole nodded. He probably knew all of this, but they were saying it for my benefit. "Go back to the hotel and wait. We'll have someone come to you with the flash drive. Room number?"

Cole gave them the hotel address and the room number. "They can be trusted?"

"They can. But if you want to take extra steps?"

"Yes," Cole said. "Do it. We'll be ready for you."

Jude cleared his throat. "Less than an hour if we can make it work. Absolutely no more than two."

"Got it."

Cole hung up, and I stared at him. "Extra steps?"

"We can't have someone walk into the hotel and go straight up to our room. They said they're watching, and we don't know what that means or whether they have people with current access to the security footage. The guys will have it put in something for room service. Or maintenance. Whatever will raise the least suspicion."

I took in one slow breath through my nose. "What if they know?"

Pressing his forehead to mine, he closed his eyes. "We'll pray they don't. This is the only option we have, Rayne. And I promise you, *I promise you*, we're going to do everything we can to get your mother and sister back, okay?"

Never in my life had I been this afraid. Not when there was the man in my house, and not when we hid behind the rocks. Not even when Ava fell out of the tree and we waited to see what kind of damage had been done to her body.

"Do you believe me?" he asked.

"Yes."

I did believe him. Cole had followed through on everything he'd said he would do. Including back when we were dealing with Simon and the Riders. Had he gone about it the wrong way? Yes. But Emma and Daniel were here because of him. They had a child because of him. He protected me and saved me, and he was doing everything he could to hold me together right now. I believed him.

"Call the driver. He can't know anything's wrong."

Nodding, I called him and told him our visit had been shorter than expected. No signs of suspicion. He would be here in five minutes.

"Look at me," Cole said gently. With infinite tenderness, he wiped my tears away from under my eyes with his thumbs. Then the rest of my face.

"Am I a mess?"

He shook his head. "No. You're not. You've never been a mess, Rayne, and you're not now. Feeling fear and emotion isn't being a mess—it's being human. You're okay. And as soon as we're back in the hotel, you can fall apart for as long as you need to."

I leaned on his shoulder and followed his lead into the car, not saying anything. If I opened my mouth, I might crumble, and lives depended on my not doing that. Once we were in the hotel, I could fall apart.

At least, until we had to leave.

*Hold on*, I prayed the words, sending them toward wherever Mom and Ava were. *We're coming.*

## Chapter 29

**Cole**

ALMOST AN HOUR after we got back to the hotel, we heard a knock on the door from room service. A handsome, dark-skinned man stood outside the door with a tray. A container of coffee and what looked like a spread of fruit and chocolate.

He had the look I recognized—ex-military or current military. The way he held himself, alert and ready, this guy knew what he was doing. The warrior in me recognized the warrior in him.

"You ordered room service?"

"We did, thank you."

"You're welcome." His eyes flicked down to the napkin on the tray, and he nodded as I took it from him.

I shut the door and placed the tray on the desk. Rayne was in the bathroom washing her face. She'd fallen apart when we came back, and I didn't blame her. This was her worst fear, and if anything happened to her mother or sister, it would lock that fear and devastation into her for the rest of her life.

The napkin held the flash drive. It looked nearly identical to the first one, and I hoped that whoever we were about to turn it over to didn't have the feel and weight of the other one memorized.

Rayne came out of the bathroom, her eyes red but dry. I held up the flash drive. "Got it."

"Okay."

I pulled her against me again, unable to stand the look of pain on her face. God, I was so fucking in love with this woman I couldn't breathe. But this wasn't the time to tell her. She was already going through so much. Adding the expectation of a first "I love you," right now? No.

When I told her I loved her, I wanted it to be with nothing else in between us.

"You ready to go?" I asked quietly.

"Do I need anything special to go on a clandestine kidnapping exchange?"

I smiled into her hair. "No. We've got the flash drive." I tucked the small device into the back pocket of her jeans. "So, you're ready to go."

"Then let's get this over with," she said. "I just want it to be done."

"Me too." I tilted her face up to mine and kissed her. "You're incredible."

"I don't feel incredible."

"Doesn't mean you're not."

We had our phones and the drive. I pulled the hotel door closed behind us. This was one of the hotels that spanned an entire block, so it was easy to go out the back of the hotel and avoid the Bureau protection we'd been assigned. He relied on us to tell him when we were going anywhere, so I wasn't concerned.

Rayne's hand in mine, I hailed a cab. I had already looked up where we needed to go, and I'd picked an address near to it so we could get out and walk. Getting an innocent cab driver to drop you off at the exact location of a clandestine exchange was asking for trouble.

I opened the door to the cab for Rayne, and across the street, I saw the man who'd delivered the flash drive to us. You wouldn't think anything of it passing by him, just leaning against one of the buildings, scrolling on his phone. Maybe waiting for a friend, maybe looking for directions.

Making sure not to stare at him, I helped Rayne into the car, and the man and I made eye contact briefly. What he could do for us now, I didn't know, but I felt better having an ally, however flimsy.

We gave the intersection address to the driver, and he took off. Rayne was quiet. What could we talk about other than what we were about to do? And we couldn't say anything in front of the driver.

Rayne kept biting her bottom lip, a sure sign of her nerves. I was just as anxious as she was, but I didn't show it. She needed me to be the steady one right now. When this was over—and it *would* be over—I would spend time telling her about my fears, so she understood I wasn't unaffected by this.

"Tell me about Rudy's," I said, by way of distraction.

She startled, shaking her head out of the fog of thoughts. "Um, it's one of those places where you go in and order at the counter and then pick up the food. The big one in the city has all kinds of arcade games and pool tables. But they make a really good burger. You would like it."

"I'm sure I would." I squeezed her hand.

The cab pulled up to the corner where we'd asked, a few blocks away from the construction site we were headed to.

I paid the driver, and Rayne wiped the sweat off her hands on her jeans, checking her back pocket.

My phone chimed. I pulled it out to turn it off and saw it

was a text from Jared Warwick, my acquaintance at the Seattle field office.

*Heard you're in the clear. You looking to come back here?*

IF YOU ARE, *let me know. I'll be sure to put in a good word for you.*

I couldn't even think about that right now, given we were about to walk into an abandoned building to meet with Thomas Peretti's men.

A thought slipped into my head. We knew where Thomas Peretti's men were. They were going to meet us. We had a copy of the files they wanted. It would be so easy to get these assholes arrested with evidence in their hands.

Handing over these kinds of people would secure my position at the Bureau for years to come—and hand me one hell of a career. No matter what had happened in the past, it would bump me on to the fast track for other things.

A year ago, I would have pulled the trigger on doing it without a second thought. My life with the Bureau and my pursuit of revenge and justice were all that mattered.

Now? If I called in the Bureau, the chances of Rayne's family dying went through the roof. She would never forgive me, and I would never forgive myself.

No. I was choosing her because I loved her. That was worth so much more than a job. Worth so much more than anything.

Switching my phone to silent, I put it away. I still hadn't decided what I was going to do as far as the Bureau, but Jared could wait.

"Let's go." I took Rayne's hand, the two of us walking in silence.

This was the kind of construction site you didn't wander around. It looked sinister, and you wouldn't want to be caught here after dark. They hadn't given us instructions on where to go, so I assumed it wouldn't be too complicated.

Thankfully, it wasn't.

We pushed through a gap in some plastic sheeting, and Rayne gasped. "Oh my god."

Across the cavernous space, we saw five men, along with an older woman and a younger woman in a wheelchair. A few cars were parked behind them. Rayne's mother and sister. One man held the handle of Ava's wheelchair, and another had a hold on the mother's arm, a gun pointed at her side. From here, they looked okay. Shaken, but okay. I tightened my hand on Rayne's, keeping her from dashing forward.

No sudden movements. All the men were packing.

"Glad you could make it," the man in the center said. He wore a slick suit, and his stance was casual. This was someone used to being obeyed. "My name is Antonio. It's nice to finally meet you, Rayne Westerfield."

"I can't say the same."

God, I loved this woman.

The guys who'd roughed up the cabin had mentioned an Antonio. He must be high up in Peretti's organization.

Antonio spread his hands. "We have nothing against you. We simply want our property back."

"You'll get it," I said. "Send them over, and I'll bring you the drive."

"No." His eyes fell on me. "I'm willing to let them come to you, but Rayne will bring me the flash drive. She's the one who had it. She's the one who will return it. As it should be."

I opened my mouth, and Rayne squeezed my hand. "It's okay, Cole. As long as they're safe, I'll do it."

"You should let me," I whispered.

"Clearly, they're not going to go for it, and I'm not negotiating with my family's lives." She looked at Antonio. "Fine. But they come here first. As a gesture of goodwill."

He smirked but inclined his head. The henchmen holding Rayne's mom let her go, and she jolted forward, shoving the other man away from Ava and pushing the wheelchair toward us. In that simple movement, I saw where Rayne got her strength. A gun pointed at her, and her mom still shoved one of them.

Rayne waited until they were almost to us before she rushed forward, wrapping her mom and then her sister, into her arms. "I'm so sorry," I heard her say. "I'm so sorry."

"We're okay," her mom said. "We're fine."

"I'm waiting, Rayne," Antonio called.

I glared at him. "You took her family. Give her a fucking minute."

Rayne pushed the wheelchair all the way to me and turned. Catching her hand, I pulled her close. "Come back to me." My words were nothing but a breath. "I'm not done with you, princess."

"It'll be fine." Her smile didn't reach her eyes.

She walked away from me, and everything about it felt wrong. She shouldn't be the one putting herself in danger. And there *was* danger. I didn't trust these men at all.

"Is she going to be okay?" Rayne's sister asked.

I could lie and say yes, but anything could happen. "I hope so."

Rayne pulled the flash drive out of her back pocket and handed it to him. "Here. Happy?"

He grabbed her shoulder and held her back from returning. "Not so fast, Miss Westerfield. You don't mind if we check this, do you?"

The belittling, oily tone in his voice made me sick. My hands curled into fists. He had his *hands on her*. One of the other guys grabbed a laptop from the car and put it on the hood. Antonio walked her over to the computer and put in the flash drive. Everything hurt from the tension in my body, holding myself still.

He clicked a few times and turned to Rayne. "I thought I made myself clear." His gun was out and pointed at her head in less than a second. "You weren't to involve the FBI."

Ava and her mother screamed, and I heard a rushing in my ears. It took everything in me not to run to her. She would be dead long before I reached her.

"We didn't," Rayne said. Her voice didn't waver for a second. "But the real one is hidden. I'm the only one here who knows where it is. They don't know, and I'll only tell you once you let them go. All of them."

"Rayne," I called.

*No.* This couldn't happen. If they took her, there was no guarantee I would ever see her again.

"And what makes you think I won't just shoot you and then them?" Antonio asked. "If you're the only one who knows where it is, then maybe it should stay lost."

The gun touched her forehead. I was going to lose it, sprint for her, and damn the consequences. "I'm the only one *here* who knows where it is," Rayne said.

She was so fucking smart, and if she got out of this alive, I was going to kill her. The one thing going for us was these guys clearly *didn't* know we'd already turned over the real thing.

"Let them go," Rayne said. "Or I'm not saying anything."

Antonio narrowed his eyes. I saw the thoughts on his face, weighing his options. The drive, and his boss's freedom, won. "Fine. But you're going to tell me, Miss Westerfield. I don't care if it has to be painful."

He looked at us. "Get out of here."

"Rayne, don't do this," I begged her. No way could I walk away from here without her by my side.

She turned, agony in her eyes. One of the men grabbed her arms, twisting them painfully behind her back. Red covered my vision, but as soon as I moved, they would put a bullet in her head.

"Take care of them and make sure they're okay," she said. Now her voice wavered, eyes flicking to her family and back to me. "I love you."

My heart dropped out of my chest and shattered on the ground. I should have told her in the hotel room. And I couldn't bear to say it for real now. But I did. "I love you."

The words were low. No one could hear them but me. Still, she saw me say them, her shoulders slumping in relief.

Antonio pulled her away and put her in one of the cars. The other men retreated and followed, the squeal of tires echoing and fading into silence. I didn't even realize my hand was gripping Ava's wheelchair so tightly my knuckles were white until they were gone.

"Oh god," Ava said, eyes teary. "Are they going to kill her? They're going to kill her, aren't they?"

"Not if I can help it," I said. "Let's get you guys out of here and safe."

And once they were okay? I was going after Rayne.

I told Rayne I wasn't a hero, and I wasn't. But for her, I would be.

Because Antonio had just made me a villain, and he had no idea what was coming.

# Chapter 30

**Cole**

I SAT in a chair in the waiting room at the hospital. Ava and her mother were being looked over, and the hospital staff were suspicious about what brought them in at all. They were doing as well as they could be, getting checked out through their tears.

Not the circumstances I'd wanted to meet them under.

I hadn't called anyone yet. The Bureau couldn't know until I had more information. They would lock me out and not tell me what was happening. The cops too. If Antonio and the rest of Peretti's men saw cops, Rayne was dead.

Dialing, I held the phone up to my ear, forcing myself to sit still and not tear out of here in a blind fury. The phone rang, and Jude picked up on the third ring. "Cole."

"Please tell me you put something on the flash drive." My voice sounded like it had been dragged over a hundred miles of gravel. "Something to trace it. Like a backward worm?"

"What happened?" Lucas's voice sounded through the phone.

I told them, trying to contain my anger and fear, keeping my voice rational. It didn't fool them.

Daniel cleared his throat. "How are you holding up?"

"I want to burn the fucking world down," I growled.

Jude laughed once. "Sounds about right. To answer your question, yes, I did put a tracker in there. I got a ping when they looked at the drive. But I can't give you a direction until the laptop is active again."

My gut fell. "Shit."

"But we can do you one better," Lucas said.

"Tell me."

"Our man who delivered the drive to you. His name is David. He hasn't checked in yet, but we were waiting."

I nodded, though they couldn't see me. "I saw him outside the hotel when we left for the meet."

"He was instructed to tail you and keep tailing in case anything happened. I'll loop him in."

"Jude—" I cut off. "All of you. Thank you."

"We've all been through this," Daniel said. "You saw it with me. All of us have had a moment like this. Rayne is part of the family. We're not letting her go without a fight."

A crackle came through on the line. "Hey, Resting Warrior."

"David," Jude said, and everyone on the call suddenly went silent and focused on the new element in the conversation. "Tell me."

"They took the woman. Tossed her phone as soon as they left the initial site. They pulled a divide and conquer. I lost the car, but I'll find it again."

"You what?" I asked.

He went quiet, and I heard a shift in his tone. "Are you and the family secure?"

"The family is secure. Wherever you end up, that's where I'll be."

"Not a good idea."

Rage seethed beneath my skin. "I swear to god—"

"Cole," Daniel said. "Stop. We didn't have a chance to swap histories. David, Cole knows what he's doing. Let us know when you find the location and you have an assessment."

"Will do." He hung up.

"I'm going."

Lucas chuckled. "We know. David has equipment you'll need. We'll get whatever we can when he sends the address, and we can help try to guide you through it."

"Do you trust this guy?" I asked. The fact that he was with them was a good endorsement, but I still didn't know him.

"He was in my unit," Lucas said. "He's a good guy, Cole. He'll help you get her back."

I sighed. "Thanks."

"Take care of the family, and when we know, you'll know. Get there. We'll tell David to hold for you."

"I have to call the Bureau on the way. Because of the drive."

"Understood." Daniel's voice came over the line. "David has earpieces as well. We'll talk when you get there."

I clicked the phone off, and a new voice spoke. "You're going to get her?"

I looked up and met the gaze of Rayne's mother standing in the doorway. "I am. As soon as I know where."

She looked behind her, down the hall where Ava was still being looked after by nurses. "Be honest with me, please. Is my daughter already dead?"

"No." I shook my head. "Not yet."

"And do you really think you can get her back?"

Taking a breath, I fought the pain in my chest. "I can't promise that. When Thomas Peretti is involved, no one can promise anything. But I can tell you I love your daughter, and I will do anything I can to get her back. *Anything*."

She looked at me for a long moment, like she needed to know if I was telling the truth. Finally, she nodded. "Please help her."

"I will."

But every moment I didn't have an address was a moment my fear grew. Ava and her mom got checked out, and when it was confirmed they were fine, I still had no information. Jude relayed via text that we were still in the dark.

We went back to their apartment. "I'm sorry it's such a mess."

"It could be worse," Rayne's mother said. "We could be dead."

Dread pooled in the pit of my stomach. It had been three hours since Rayne had been taken. Going on four. The longer it went, the lower the chances were of getting her back, and losing her *wasn't an option*.

My phone chimed. An address.

"Is that them?"

"Yes." I was at the door in seconds. "They're not going to come back for you, but barricade the door anyway. Don't open it for anyone."

I didn't wait to hear her say she would, ducking out of the apartment and jogging to the elevator. I needed a cab. The pin Jude dropped told me the location was half an hour away. Too long. It was too long.

*Fuck.*

I dialed the internal number for the Chicago field office. "Chicago field office. How may I direct your call?"

"This is Special Agent Cole Phillips. I need to speak to Special Agent Bordeaux right now. It's urgent."

"Hold please."

A cab pulled over to the curb, and I slid into the back, rattling the address off to the driver. "I need to get there as quickly as possible. I'm with the FBI. Break whatever traffic laws you can without getting arrested. It's a matter of life and death."

The guy raised his eyebrows. "Yeah, okay."

I flipped the phone to the speaker just as Bordeaux came on. "This is Special Agent Bordeaux."

"It's Phillips," I said.

"Phillips. You ready to come off leave already?"

Returning the driver's look, I flipped it off speaker, and he inclined his head. He believed me now. And we were speeding. "No. I'm calling about something else. Thomas Peretti's man Antonio kidnapped Rayne Westerfield's mother and sister. They're safe now, but he has Rayne."

He cleared his throat. "What?"

"You heard me. This is happening now."

"Where are they located?"

I repeated the address, watching the streets fly by and the driver speed up when I said the word "kidnapped."

"That's a known compound. Less security than some of their others, because it's a place they're not afraid to abandon. There's no way to get in there alone."

That was code for they did things at the location they didn't want to deal with at their permanent properties. "I'm not alone," I said.

"Phillips, do not engage Peretti's men. Stand down. We'll get a team together, make sure we have all the information, and keep you posted. There are certain things we can't do because of the court case. The trial is starting next week."

Familiar rage boiled up, and this time, I embraced it. "I may not be fully read in on the case, but I know enough about these people to know they're going to hurt her. So, no, I'm not going to stand down. The woman I love is in danger, and I'm going to go get her, no matter the cost. This is a courtesy call, letting you know it's happening.

"If you want any part of this rescue, you need to get off your asses *now*. Got it?"

I hung up without hearing his answer. He could make whatever decision he wanted to, but that was up to him. Telling me to stand down wasn't going to happen.

"Sorry for not believing you."

"I wouldn't believe me either," I said. "Just get me there."

"Working on it."

Leaning forward, I dropped my head into my hands and tried to breathe. Only a thread was holding me together right now. One snap and everything would come spilling out.

I couldn't think about Rayne in pain or danger. All I could do was find the inner focus I used to have while in the Navy. Or on missions. Nothing else. And I would get her back.

"Here we go."

We'd gotten here in half the time. I gave him a hundred-dollar tip on top of the rest of it. "Thank you."

"Good luck."

David stood by a sedan in an alley, sizing me up. "You sure you want to do this?"

"Did they tell you who I am?"

He smirked and held out an earpiece. "No, but with that walk and the look in your eyes, I know I'm not going to change your mind."

"Good." I looked in his trunk, cataloging the range of weapons, both lethal and nonlethal. "How did you find them?"

"I know their safe houses. I had to check them until I saw the car they put her in. It took time, especially if I didn't want to be noticed casing all their properties. These guys don't mess around."

I didn't bother asking how he knew about mafia safe houses. It wasn't any of my business, and based on the kind of company we all kept, he could have any number of reasons.

Quickly, I put in the earpiece. "Hello?"

"Hey," Jude said. "Everyone's here and listening, but I'll be the one talking and guiding you. I have the schematics of the building, but I don't know where people will be or where she's being held."

"What's it look like?"

David picked up a handgun and slid it into a holster on his belt, adding extra magazines to the other side. He handed me a bulletproof vest, and I strapped it on.

"Three stories, looks like an older-style office building."

"Take what you want," David said.

There were various guns, a taser, and a baton. "I don't have a badge at the moment."

"Neither do they," David pointed out. "And they won't hesitate to shoot first."

I picked up the other handgun and checked the magazine, taking a couple more as well. "I've informed the FBI. I have no idea if they're going to help. I wasn't on the phone long after they told me to stand down and I told them to fuck off."

David chuckled, and Jude said, "Damn."

"That plan in Montana is looking like a well-oiled machine at this point, right, Daniel?" I was referencing our wild helicopter ride and improvised attempt to get Emma back from her deranged drug lord of a father.

Jude confirmed. "He said yes," Jude confirmed.

My phone buzzed, the number for the field office appearing. I slid the call on. "If you're calling to tell me to stand down again—"

"Teams will be there in ten minutes," Bordeaux said.

I glanced at David. "Someone will be waiting here to receive you. His name is David. He'll direct you."

"Noted."

David's face went rigid with anger as I ended the call. "I'm not staying here."

"Ten minutes. Please."

Jude spoke in our ears. "David, I've got him with this one. Stay there and wait for the FBI."

He didn't look happy about it, but he leaned down into the truck and handed me a suppressor. "Try not to die."

"I'll do my best."

Turning to the end of the alley, I took a deep breath. "Talk to me, Jude."

"Easiest entrance is on the east side. Down the alley. The hallway is small there, not a lot of room for traffic."

"What kind of security are we thinking?" I screwed the silencer onto the barrel of the gun, my mind sinking into a cool place of calm. "I was told it shouldn't be too bad."

"I think it'll be worse on the inside."

Plastering myself against the wall, I glanced around the corner toward the alley Jude mentioned. The building itself was nondescript. Walking past it, you'd never know it was anything other than an office building or an abandoned structure. A few cars were parked in the alley, including one I recognized. I saw the entrance door, with a camera above it.

I needed to move fast.

Turning, I swung my arm up and around the corner, taking out the camera. My body moved on instinct, running into the alley and evaluating the lock. Code lock. I skidded to a stop and shot through it, kicking in the door. The guy standing inside barely had time to react. As I slammed the gun into his temple, he dropped like a rock. I took his gun, released the magazine, and tossed the body into the alley behind one of the cars.

The hallway was small, like Jude said, no one else in sight. "I'm in," I said. "I took out one of the cameras, so I don't have long."

"I only have the plans the city had on file. I don't know any modifications they made. So I can guide you, but you won't be completely informed."

"It's fine." I yanked the belt out of the guy's pants and secured his wrists quickly. "Let's just hope there's not a cluster of them."

Footsteps came toward me, running. Two sets. Someone slammed around the corner, and I fired, taking down the first one. The second, I shot in the knee, hitting him in the head too. I kept one of their guns and ditched the other one.

"Three down."

I glanced around the corner, and it was clear, looking like a normal building so far.

"The FBI is on-site," David said, voice crackling in my ear. "We'll follow you ASAP."

"Okay," I said.

But I wasn't stopping. Rayne needed me, and absolutely nothing was going to stand in my way.

# Chapter 31

**Rayne**

WHEN I HEARD ABOUT TORTURE—AND I heard about it a fair amount in my line of work, assisting veterans and service members with PTSD—this wasn't the kind of room I imagined.

It looked like an office from the '80s. Stained walls, popcorn ceiling, musty smell. The carpet was covered with plastic sheeting, which didn't help the fear coursing through my veins. They had me strapped to a dentist's chair, or close enough, and had left me alone.

The tray of implements nearby left no questions about why I was here. But at least they hadn't started right away.

Antonio strode in, rolling up the sleeves on his button-down shirt, the suit jacket long gone. "Where is it?"

I shook my head. "I don't know."

He sighed, but it seemed more resigned than angry. "I figured as much. Should have killed you back at the meetup, but I think you *do* know where it is, and one body is easier to deal with than four."

Pulling on blue plastic gloves, Antonio picked up a scalpel. "I could go straight to the really hard stuff, but I don't think we'll need it. You're going to tell me where the real flash drive is, and every time I have to ask, this is going to get worse."

"If I tell you, you're just going to kill me anyway. What's the point?"

He shook his head. "It doesn't have to be that way. If you're giving us back something we need, it's enough. Crossing us is a different matter, but we both know you were never supposed to have the drive, let alone see what was on it."

Antonio put one hand on my shoulder, pressing it back into the chair, and fire slashed across my arm, the meat of the muscle. I screamed, unable to stop myself.

Hearing about torture was one thing. Living through it was another. Jude had survived this for months? How?

My body fought the restraints, trying to get away. A second line of fire spread beneath the first, and it went on forever.

"Where is it?"

I needed to hold on until Cole found me. Because he would. He and the FBI would come and find me. I *had* crossed them by doing this meet. "I don't know."

My voice wasn't recognizable. Even to myself. I'd never sounded like this before.

"If you think this is the most painful it can get, Miss West-erfield, I'm sorry to say you're mistaken."

New pain struck the other side of my body. This time in my hand. In between my fingers. I was blind with it—I couldn't even see what he was doing. All I knew was I needed to make it stop. Sobs and screams came out of me. I wasn't a soldier. I didn't know how to withstand pain like this.

*Nor should you have to.* It was Cole's voice in my head. *Just stay alive, princess.*

"Where is the flash drive, Rayne?"

"It's too late." I forced the words out. "It's already too late."

Shame overcame me at how easily I was giving in to them. But I felt the blood running down my arms and in between my fingers. "You can't get it back."

Antonio grabbed my jaw and forced me to look at him. "What are you saying?"

"The FBI already has the drive." I swallowed back another groan of pain. "It was with them before you even took my family. They already know everything, and there's no way to undo it."

Shattering pain cracked through my face so quickly, it took me a second to realize he'd hit me. He got right in my vision, his face now so calm it was more frightening than anything else. "See, that's what you should have kept to yourself, Rayne. Because until this moment, you were a victim in all of this. An unfortunate case of collateral damage who probably could have come out of this all right. But now?"

He shook his head, going back to the tray of implements. "Now, you've crossed us. And as I said before, no one can do that and go unpunished."

"Please." I wasn't above begging. "Your boss is already in jail. This won't come back on you. I didn't see anything on the drive that can help him. You'll never hear from or see me again. I swear it."

Metal rattled as he looked through the tools. "That doesn't matter. Just because Peretti is in jail doesn't mean the rules don't apply. Even if he goes to jail forever, he's still in charge, and we have a reputation and our own laws to uphold. And if I let you go, then everyone will think they can get away with shit like this.

"I can't let that stand, even if you getting the flash drive was an accident. We need examples to keep people in line.

You'll join Susan White six feet below the ground. You helped her live a few hours longer, but she tried to be a hero too, and look where that got her."

"You don't have to do this. Please." Panic sliced through me and cut me down to my barest instincts. Survival. Antonio had pliers in his hands, and I didn't know what he meant to do with them, whether it was my teeth or my fingers, but I wasn't going to *let* him do it.

I thrashed against the restraints, screaming at the top of my lungs. If I was going out, then I was going out fighting. He grabbed my jaw again, hard enough to bruise. "This will hurt more if you don't stay still."

He suddenly shouted, falling away from me. I heard more shouting and gunshots coming from everywhere, chaos and noise I couldn't process with so much adrenaline and fear running through my system. Something heavy covered me. I fought as much as I could, trying to get it off. "Get it off, *get it off*!" I yelled.

"It's me, princess. It's me."

"Cole?"

"I'm right here." His body pressed into mine. "I'm covering you until it's over, okay? I'm wearing a vest."

Everything collapsed around me. He was here. He was here. He'd come for me.

"*Stay on the ground!*" a voice yelled.

My whole body shook. "You came for me."

It was still the only thought in my mind, even though I'd known he would try. Feeling the end come close and getting a reprieve changed you. Now I understood so much more of what some of my patients had gone through.

Cole pulled back, his face close to mine. "Of course I fucking came for you. I love you."

My heart both soared and fluttered inside my chest. I'd seen him mouth the words, but that was nothing compared to

224

hearing them up close. "I love you," I told him. "I'm sorry I had to do it. I didn't want to. I just needed them to be safe."

Cole slipped a hand behind my neck and kissed me hard. "I know. They're safe and fine. And I'm sorry for not getting here sooner." His hands moved to the restraints, getting them off me. "We need to get you to the hospital."

"I'm okay. You got here before he could do any major damage."

Looking behind him, he called to someone. "Are we clear?"

"Yeah."

Cole stripped off the bulletproof vest then his T-shirt, ripping it in half. He wrapped part of it around my arm and the rest around my bleeding hand. "I was still too late, princess. He never should have been able to touch you."

I threw my arms around him as soon as I was free, clinging to him. He lifted me out of the chair and pulled me away from it, scooping an arm under my legs so he held me. Just like when he'd saved me out in the snow.

Antonio was still on the ground, glaring at me, blood coming from a wound in his leg.

"We listened," Cole said quietly. "I came in alone, but the FBI caught up. He'd already hurt you, and he was talking. So, we listened, and he confessed to murder in front of about fifteen FBI agents. He's going to jail."

"Good." I let my head fall against his shoulder, the adrenaline leaving me and bringing exhaustion and more pain in its wake.

Carrying me out into the hallway and away from the chair and the blood, Cole sank to his knees. "I'll bring you to the ambulance. Promise," he said. "I just need a minute."

He held me so tightly I could barely breathe, his own emotions shaking him. "That's the second time I almost lost you," he whispered. "It's not going to happen again."

I pulled his mouth down to mine, not knowing what to say

or how to say it. We would both come out of this with scars, mental and physical. My own fears about my loved ones—and probably new ones related to all that we'd just been through together. Cole's fear about not making it in time to save me, just like he hadn't been able to save his brother.

Cole sucked in a shaky breath. "I couldn't let it in. Not really. Because if I did, I wouldn't have been able to focus enough to get to you." He pressed his forehead to mine. "I love you," he said again. "I thought about saying it to you earlier in the hotel room, and I'll forever regret *not* saying it. I didn't want to pile on to your emotions. And then you said it, and I think my soul left my body."

Burying my face in his neck, I breathed him in. The idea of resisting this now was unthinkable. Cole had been right from the beginning—something brought us together in a way I couldn't explain, and I'd forever be grateful for it.

"Let's get you looked at," he finally said. "Because I need to hold you for a lot longer than this."

I nodded, melting against his body as he lifted me and carried me down and out of the building to the waiting ambulance. It was easier to breathe now, knowing he would never let me go.

# Chapter 32

**Cole**

MY CHEST FELT TIGHT, and I knew it wouldn't ease until Rayne was back in my arms. But the doctors and nurses were with her now, getting her fixed up. Her wounds weren't serious, which I was eternally grateful for.

It had been way, *way* too close.

When they'd pulled me back to wait for the asshole to confess, I'd nearly lost myself in the raw anger of needing to get to her.

Scrubbing a hand over my face, I leaned against the wall by her door, waiting for them to be finished with her.

"Phillips," a voice boomed.

I turned and found Special Agent Bordeaux coming toward me. "Sir. You're here with the prisoners?"

"Yeah."

They needed to get checked out and treated before they went to lockup. The ones who were still alive anyway.

"She all right?"

"She will be," I said. I would make sure of it.

Bordeaux clapped me on the shoulder. "You did good, Phillips. When you get back, we have plenty of things for you to work on. You won't be bored, that's for sure."

I cleared my throat. "Sir, I won't be returning."

"I was afraid of that. Seattle is clamoring for you too. Can't say I blame them."

"No, sir. I mean I won't be returning at all. After my admin leave is over, I'd like to retire."

The man's face went slack. "What the hell are you talking about, Phillips?"

What was I talking about?

Glancing toward Rayne's room, I smiled. Everything in me felt settled and grounded. Something I hadn't felt in years, maybe ever. "I've found where I needed to be, sir. It's not with the Bureau. I've contributed to situations like this for too long, and now I'd like to help people recover from them."

He snorted. "That ranch out in Montana? Seriously?"

"Seriously. They do incredible work. Work more than one agent could benefit from."

"Well," he said. "You're one hell of an agent, and I think you're making a mistake. But I can't stop you." Holding out his hand, he sighed. "Thank you for your work. I'll make sure everything goes through for you. Enjoy the rest of your leave. You've definitely earned your pay on that one."

I laughed once, but my stomach clenched. Rayne and I both would have wanted things to have gone differently. And yet, if it hadn't happened the same way, would we still be here? Together?

There was no way to know.

"Thank you." I shook his hand. "I'll be in touch."

"Cole," Ava called from down the hallway, wheeling faster than her mother walking behind her. Bordeaux inclined his head and left while they took his place. "Is she—"

"She's okay," I said. "I'll let her tell you the rest. It's her story. I think they're almost done with her, but you should be able to go in."

Ava narrowed her eyes. "Why are you out here?"

"Just giving the doctors some space." I smiled tightly. "And I'm not family." *Yet*, I said in my mind.

"We'll see about that," her mother muttered, taking Ava's chair and marching into the room with a look that told me she wasn't having any of it.

"Oh my *god*." Ava's voice floated out the door. I smiled. Her mom and sister were lovely, and I looked forward to seeing them more. If they needed help to repair the apartment, I would be there for that too.

I pulled out my phone and made a call. As soon as the breaching had been complete, the guys at the ranch had signed off. I knew they'd be waiting for an update, and I had a question for them too.

Daniel answered. "Good to hear from you," he said.

"She's alive. Superficial injuries. We're at the hospital now."

Jude blew out a breath. "That's good news we will happily pass on. Everyone here has been worried."

I knew enough about the Resting Warrior women to understand they would know about this already. They knew their men better than they knew themselves, and something this big? They would know.

"Tell them she's all right. I think we'll stay here a few more days to make sure and help her mom and sister get their apartment back together."

Daniel chuckled. "You've got plenty of that kind of work to do back here. But we're going to help you."

Swallowing, I fought the nerves in my gut. "I have a question for you guys."

"What's up?"

"Well." I took a deep breath. "I just told the FBI I didn't want to come back after my leave. And what all of this has shown me is I'd rather be on the other side of it. I know I still have a lot of work to do with your trust, but—"

"Cole," Jude said, stopping me. "No one questions you. We can see it."

"And yes. Absolutely, you have a place here. With the way things are changing around here, we need the extra set of hands," Daniel said.

"Thank you." The nerves fell out of me, and I gave the wall more of my weight. Hearing them say yes and that they trusted me meant more than I let on.

"Take care of Rayne, and we'll see you when you're back."

"Sounds good. We'll keep you posted."

I hung up and closed my eyes, the last of my stress melting away. I wasn't going to be living in Jimmy's cabin anymore, but that didn't matter. I'd find a place. I'd move in with Rayne if she'd have me or build her a new place if she wanted.

"Cole, get in here," I heard Ava calling me.

The nurses were gone, and it was just the three of them in the room. "Hey."

"Hey." Rayne watched me. She was in a hospital gown and had bandages around one arm, all around her hand, and bruises were forming on her face. The fucker had sliced her in between her fingers. I wished I'd shot him somewhere more important than his leg, but my only thought had been to disable him without hitting Rayne.

"We're going to go," Rayne's mother said.

"You just got here," I said. "Are you sure?"

She looked at her daughter. "Yeah. I hope you guys will stay a few more days?"

"Definitely. I still need to try Rudy's."

"Fuck yes, you do," Ava said.

"*Language.*"

Ava just smirked and wheeled herself past me, stopping briefly. "Thank you. And not just for this. You're good for her."

I looked back up at Rayne. "She's good for me too."

Rayne had tears in her eyes, and she shook her head. "You guys don't have to go."

Her mom leaned over and kissed her head. "You're safe, and we'll see you as soon as you're ready. But I think you need some time. We wanted to show you we were all right."

Rayne nodded. "Okay."

They left, and I just stared at her. Like she was staring at me. "Want to get the hell out of here?"

"Yes, please."

It didn't take long to check out at the hospital. Rayne's injuries weren't severe enough for them to keep her overnight, and I wanted privacy with her.

As soon as we got to the hotel, I sat her down on one of the couches in the lobby. She was dragging, exhausted. "Stay here for a second, okay? I need to take care of something."

"Okay."

The woman at the front desk smiled at me. "How can I help you?"

"My name is Cole Phillips. I'd like to upgrade my room, please."

"Sure thing, let me just check—" She stared at the screen for a moment. "Actually, your room has already been upgraded, courtesy of your *Special Acquaintance*, and all of your things have already been moved." She slid a packet of key cards across the counter to me.

I picked up the cards and stared at her. "Really?"

"Yep! All taken care of. You have the room for…two weeks."

Holy shit. I needed to send Bordeaux a bottle of whiskey or something. "Thank you, I appreciate it."

"No problem."

Rayne looked like she was nearly falling asleep when I took her hand and pulled her to her feet. "Let's go, princess." I needed to get her upstairs and into the room so I could tell her the news and hold her the way I'd wanted to for hours now.

"Where are we?" she asked when I unlocked an incredible suite on one of the top floors.

"I went to upgrade our room, but the Bureau beat me to it. We have it for two weeks if we want it."

She wandered through the living room and into the massive bedroom. I only had eyes for her.

"Is it bad if I don't even want to put on pajamas?"

Laughing, I followed her. "I'll always be in favor of sleeping naked." Stripping my shirt over my head, I tossed it aside and undressed the rest of the way. Rayne, too, stripped off her clothes until she stood naked in front of me.

She was so beautiful—and so much more than that. "I really need to hold you right now."

"Thank god, because I need you to do that," she laughed.

I pulled the blankets back, sliding into the giant bed with Rayne and, being careful of her injuries, settled her across my chest. Rayne's fingers gripped my side, and I heard her sniffle. She hadn't let anything out yet. "It's okay," I whispered. "I've got you."

She cried, the sounds cracking my heart in two. At the same time, I was glad she could let go with me. The Rayne I'd run into in the hotel lobby weeks ago would never have let me see her cry.

When her tears ran out, I rubbed a hand up and down her back. "I'm so sorry, Rayne."

"You saved my life. You can't say sorry."

"I still am."

Her breathing eased, and I couldn't fight my smile. "I have something to tell you."

"Please let it be something good."

"I think it's good."

She turned so she could see me, and I reached out to brush some remaining tears off her face. "I'm not going back to the FBI. After my leave is over, I'm taking retirement."

Rayne gasped. "Cole."

"And I spoke to Daniel. He offered me a place at Resting Warrior."

"Really?" The hope in her eyes was too much to bear.

I kissed her. "Really. I don't want to be anywhere else. The community there, and you, that's what I want from my life. Not diving into danger or putting people in it."

She turned and climbed over me, kissing me in a way that would not have us resting. "If this is some kind of joke, I can't take it, Cole. This is real?"

Sliding one hand behind her neck, I pulled her down to me again. "It's real, princess. I love you, and I'm not leaving. I'll find a place to live that's not the cabin. If you're not ready to live with me, it's okay. If you want to live in your house together, that's okay too. If you want to burn it to the ground and build a new one, I'll do it. It might take me a while, but I'll do it."

"I want to live with you," she said. "I don't know where—I don't think I'll know how I feel about the house until I get back to it. But I want to be with you. Preferably in a house that has both heat and power."

"I agree. But I request wherever we live, we get both a very large bed and a very large bathtub."

Her eyes lit up. "I like the sound of that." Then her face softened. "I have something to tell you too. Given everything, I think I need to take a leave of absence. I don't know what's going to hit me or how, but I feel it lurking down there."

I brushed some hair out of her face and turned us so she was beneath me on the bed. "It's probably a good idea."

"I feel like I'm letting everyone down. I have clients who need me."

"Your clients need someone who's sure of themselves and their practice. Taking a break to take care of yourself is doing them a favor."

"Yeah."

I kissed the tip of her nose. "The fact that you feel guilty about it is something you should probably work on."

Rayne narrowed her eyes. "Trying to do my job for me?"

"Never. But you've helped a lot of people at Resting Warrior. Now it's time for them to help you."

Her eyes went glassy again, and she wrapped her arms around my neck. "You're staying with me."

"I'm staying with you, princess."

There was no way to tell who kissed the other. We simply came together, consuming each other, and writing three words back and forth across our lips. I loved Rayne Westerfield, and I couldn't wait to show her for the rest of our lives.

## Epilogue

**Rayne**

*One Month Later*

Emma bounced Tyson on her hip, trying to get him to settle down. The poor thing was overtired and making it widely known.

She looked over at me. "I'm sorry."

"Why are you apologizing?" I winked. "He's fine."

Cole's arms wrapped around my waist, and he pressed a kiss to my neck before stepping around me toward Emma. "Will you let me try?"

Cole was still cautious around Emma. I understood why, but Emma and Daniel made it clear at every opportunity they had no problem with him.

"At this point?" Emma said, handing Tyson over. "Yes."

It looked more natural than I imagined for Cole to hold the baby, turning him on his stomach over the length of one arm and rocking back and forth in a swooping motion. "This always worked for my brother."

Like magic, Tyson quieted down, and we all stared at him. The entire Resting Warrior crew was here in the lodge for the first family dinner in a while.

Daniel clapped Cole on the back. "I'm going to use that, thank you." He took his son from Cole's arms and crossed to the playpen they'd set up in the much quieter security office, where Avery was already sleeping.

Cole and a baby... It wasn't a thought I'd dwelled on before, but I liked it.

"Yes, thank you." Emma dragged her hands over her face. "I love him, but he's not a great sleeper."

"It'll get better." Evie pulled our friend into a hug. "I promise."

I went over to the bar and poured myself a glass of wine, and I grabbed a glass of whiskey for Cole. He didn't drink often, but he was nervous tonight. The tail end of the sentence reached me when I handed him the drink. "You're going to have your hands full when spring comes around," Noah said.

"No pressure."

In spite of the blizzard that had nearly killed us, construction was underway on the new building, with an estimate of getting it open next spring. Cole would be in charge of the new facility. They'd told him today, and he was understandably shocked and a bit anxious.

He would be incredible. Everyone knew it. In the few weeks since we'd come back from Chicago, he fit in like he'd always been here.

I wasn't used to seeing him nervous, but a drink might help a little.

Cole smiled at me. "Thank you."

"You're welcome." I slipped away to where Evie and the rest of them were clustered in the kitchen. "Did you pick one?"

"We did," Evie said. "It's not far from Grace, actually."

Lucas and Evie were building a house off the property. "It might take a while, but we need to move fast."

"Why?" Mara asked. She was no longer my client—I didn't have any clients right now—but I was proud of her progress. She rarely had trouble with her voice now.

Evie's hand dropped to her stomach, her face flushing. "We have a clock."

"*No*," Lena gasped, gently hitting Evie on the shoulder before wrapping her in a hug. "You didn't tell me?"

"I wanted to tell everyone," Evie laughed. "And you can't keep a secret."

Lena made a face, but we all laughed. We knew it was true. Everyone hugged Evie, and warmth filled my chest. There was so much love in this room, I could barely breathe. So much change too.

Gone were the seven men who had started this place, blindly searching for healing they couldn't articulate. They had transformed the ranch and *themselves* into something so much bigger.

"I'm going to be so pregnant in your wedding photos, Lena."

"You think I care about that?" Lena dabbed her eyes with a tissue. "I'm so excited. And I'll get to help you decorate a house. Both of you." She looked at me.

Cole and I were building a house as well. Near my old one, but more suited to what we both wanted. We were still living in my old house for the time being. It wasn't the memories of the mafia breaking in that made me want to move. It was my own fears.

The house, while lovely, was a home I'd made with walls around my heart I'd thought were unmovable. Until a man who saw through them wouldn't stop trying.

We both wanted a fresh start with the house.

Cori threw back her drink. "I'm going to be the fun aunt

237

to all your babies," she declared. "Our house will be the one they come to when they're too pissed at you to talk it out. Right, baby?" she called across the room to Grant.

He looked over. "What?"

We all laughed, and Grant smiled at his wife. The kind of look that told me they might excuse themselves early. It wouldn't be the first time.

"Me too," Kate said, raising her glass. "We'll be the ones with all the cute animals to come visit."

Liam crossed the room and wrapped himself around Mara, kissing her ear and whispering something. She closed her eyes, leaning back into him. The ring she wore on a chain around her neck caught the light. It matched the one on Liam's finger. A commitment without a wedding, which worked perfectly for them.

All around me, everyone was *happy*. And for the first time in my life, I was too. Truly and deeply. Ava and Mom saw it while we were there helping them rebuild and promising to come at Christmas.

Lena saw it the moment I'd walked into Deja Brew covered in bandages.

Hell, I saw it myself when I looked in the mirror and met my own gaze.

We were all happy, and there was something so overwhelming about it. Tears pricked my eyes, and I set down my wineglass. "Excuse me."

"You okay?" Grace asked.

"Yeah." I kept my voice light. "I just need a second."

Stepping out onto the porch, I inhaled the crisp air. Most of the snow from the blizzard had melted, but some remained, and the chill never left the air.

Everyone had surprised us when we'd come home, everything in the cabin, my office, and my home already set to rights, as best they could. There had been some things they couldn't save. But the relief of not having to go through it spoke volumes about this family. And it *was* a family.

Tears leaked out of my eyes. I didn't know why. It was all beautiful, and it brought this out of me.

The door opened behind me, and Cole stepped out. "Hey."

"Hey," I whispered.

He stood behind me, pressing me into the railing. "Why are you out here, princess?"

I smiled. The nickname had grown on me so much, I almost hated when he called me anything else.

"I was just looking at everyone, and we're all so happy. So different. It hit me in a weird way, and I didn't want to cry in front of everyone and make them all concerned."

Turning, I looked back through the window, where Harlan dipped Grace backward in some sort of dance he'd swept her up in before kissing her. Nothing but joy.

"And are you happy?" Cole asked.

I looked at him. The moon was already bright, painting him in pale shades on the porch. His eyes were serious—he really wanted to know.

"Yes," I breathed the word. "I'm happier than I ever thought I would be. *Could* be."

Cole reached his hand up, stroking his knuckles down my cheek. "You're everything, Rayne. You're my home. You weren't the thing that changed me, but you were the cause of my change. Because I saw myself in a new light and wanted to be the man who deserved you."

I caught his wrist. "You were always that man. It just got lost along the way."

"Maybe." One side of his mouth tipped up into a smile. "But I have my North Star now. I'll never get lost again."

Tears blurred my vision. Cole pulled me against him,

brushing his lips over my forehead. "I have something I want to ask you."

I laughed once, the sound coming through my tears. "I don't know if I'm fit for that right now."

"You are. Promise."

"Okay."

He smiled, and I felt it against my skin. "Would you say the two of us were a long time coming? It feels that way for me."

I nodded. Once I met Cole, it was like no one else existed, even when we weren't speaking and when I tried to push him away. Something deep inside me had kept me waiting for him.

"I'm glad you think so."

"Why?"

Cole took one step back so he could see me. "Because to me, it doesn't feel fast. It feels inevitable. There is no one else for me. I know it, and I think you do too."

I was nodding at his words until I saw him move again, lowering himself down onto one knee. The gasp that came out of me was loud in the silence. "Cole?"

"People will look at the two of us and say we're rushing. But we both know we're not." He pulled out a black box and opened it. "What do you say, princess? Marry me and build a whole new kind of happiness?"

Tears streamed down my face now. I couldn't stop them. Everything clicked together like the last piece of a puzzle I'd been trying to solve for years. "Yes." I managed to say the word. "Yes, of course."

Cole's smile lit up the night. He slid the ring on my finger and kissed me, bending me back over the railing. "I love you," he said. "More than anything."

"I love you." Then it dawned on me. "You weren't nervous about the job, were you?"

"No. I was nervous about asking you to be my wife."

*His wife.* I looked at the ring, glinting in the moonlight. "When the hell did you get a ring?"

He smirked. "I've had it since we left Chicago."

My jaw dropped, and I hit his arm. "What?"

"I needed to wait for the right moment."

"And tonight was it?"

A sparkle appeared in his eyes. "I thought so. They did too."

He tugged me back toward the door, and we walked into a room full of cheers. My friends pulled me in for hugs, and I could barely hear what they were saying because they all talked over one another.

A cake had appeared on the table, with Lena's signature flair. Grace was pouring champagne, and Kate was grabbing plates for the cake slices. Lena was in Jude's arms, her engagement ring sparkling in the firelight.

Just like mine.

Coming closer to us, Daniel smiled. "You know I'm the one who sabotaged your car that first family dinner, right, Rayne?"

My jaw dropped open, and Lena's words about all the guys being mother hens and matchmakers came to mind. I barely remembered him excusing himself during dinner. "What?"

He shrugged. "You both needed a reason to be thrown together, and it was harmless enough. Seems like I made a good bet."

"Unbelievable," I muttered. "Did you know?"

Cole shook his head. "No idea. I swear."

Daniel just smiled again and turned to face the room. "Seems like we have a few things to celebrate tonight." He picked up a glass of champagne. Everyone followed suit, even Evie, whose glass was full of orange juice.

"To new life," Daniel said, lifting his glass to Lucas and Evie. "To new responsibilities and new bonds." He raised his glass to Cole and me. "And to the future. This is the family I never knew I needed and never could have asked for."

Everyone raised their glass at that, and tears graced more than one set of eyes. I turned to Cole just as he turned to me, catching his lips. We were hardly alone in the kiss.

"I love you, princess," he whispered, making me smile.

"Forever?" I asked.

"Forever."

# Acknowledgments

A very special thanks to the Calamittie Jane Publishing editing and proofreading team:

Denise Hendrickson
Susan Greenbank
Chasidy Brooks
Tesh Elborne
Marilize Roos
Lisa at Silently Correcting Your Grammar

Thank you for your ongoing dedication for making these romantic suspense books the best they can be.

And to the creative minds at Deranged Doctor Designs who fashioned all the covers for this series and made the books so beautiful—thank you!

# Also by Josie Jade

See more info here: www.josiejade.com

**RESTING WARRIOR RANCH** (with Janie Crouch)

Montana Sanctuary

Montana Danger

Montana Desire

Montana Mystery

Montana Storm

Montana Freedom

Montana Silence

Montana Rain

**PRINCES OF FAIRYTALE, CO** (with Lena Phoenix)

Beau

Clint

Declan

Ezra

Garrett

Holden

Locke

Ramon

Sutton

Walker

## About the Author (Josie Jade)

Josie Jade is the pen name of an avid romantic suspense reader who had so many stories bubbling up inside her she had to write them!

Her passion is protective heroes and books about healing… broken men and women who find love—and themselves —again.

Two truths and a lie:
• Josie lives in the mountains of Montana with her husband and three dogs, and is out skiing as much as possible
• Josie loves chocolate of all kinds—from deep & dark to painfully sweet
• Josie worked for years as an elementary school teacher before finally becoming a full time author

Josie's books will always be about fighting danger and standing shoulder-to-shoulder with the family you've chosen and the people you love.

**Heroes exist.** Let a Josie Jade book prove it to you.

Printed in the USA
CPSIA information can be obtained
at www.ICGtesting.com
LVHW050231120124
768627LV00002B/187